D1390726

TWO-GUN TROUBLE

Heads turn when Jonah Durrell rides into Motherlode. A handsome, charming man, he is also a successful manhunter, as good with his fists as with his guns. Jonah just wants to enjoy himself at Miss Jenny's parlour-house; however, his visit is interrupted by the brutal murder of one of the girls. Someone wants Miss Jenny out of town — but she won't be pushed around. And Jonah will always help a damsel in distress. But at what cost?

GILLIAN F. TAYLOR

TWO-GUN TROUBLE

Complete and Unabridged

LINFORD
Leicester

Fir⟨...⟩ by

WORCESTERSHIRE COUNTY COUNCIL	
861	
ULVERSCROFT	31.10.07
WES	£8.99
KD	

The moral right of the author has been asserted

British Library CIP Data

Taylor, Gillian F.
  Two-gun trouble.—Large print ed.—
Linford western library
1. Western stories
2. Large type books
I. Title
823.9′14 [F]

ISBN 978–1–84617–815–3

Published by
F. A. Thorpe (Publishing)
Anstey, Leicestershire

Set by Words & Graphics Ltd.
Anstey, Leicestershire
Printed and bound in Great Britain by
T. J. International Ltd., Padstow, Cornwall

This book is printed on acid-free paper

Dedicated to:
Miss Jenny, who asked for it; to the
other Misses, who said 'yes', when
I asked if I could put them in a
brothel; and to a handsome,
brown-eyed boy.

1

Another flurry of late snow blew across the San Juan mountains of south west Colorado. A mist of white flakes danced along Cement Creek, 11,000 feet up under the grey, clouded sky. The dark forests of white-frosted pine were thinner up here, the trees huddling together in clumps, or growing at mad angles from the bare, red rocks. The snow hit two riders, crouched deep into their saddles as their horses plodded steadily along the frozen trail. The taller rider took the buffeting stoically, but his companion shuddered and reined his horse in. It stopped willingly, breathing heavily in the thin, pure air.

'Durrell!' he yelled, his breath clouding out through the folds of his muffler. 'Durrell, stop, damn you!'

Jonah Durrell turned his horse, a fine dapple grey that blended so perfectly

1

with the snow and clouds that it seemed a creature of the air itself.

'Let's quit this foolishness and go back to Silverton,' McReadie said, banging one hand against his thigh to try and restore circulation.

Durrell frowned; between his red muffler and the black hat, pulled down low, about the only parts of his face visible were his liquid, dark eyes. 'I came out to get Spencer, and I intend to do so,' he replied, his clipped, New England accent clear even through his muffler.

'Aw, hell,' McReadie protested. 'Let's quit and get someplace warm.'

'He beat Red Pearl almost to death,' Durrell answered, his eyes glinting with disgust. 'I aim to track him down and bring him back to pay for it.'

McReadie shrugged, the movement almost hidden under his wolf-skin coat. 'She's a whore; it happens to them.'

'Whore or not, there's no call to beat a woman,' Durrell said fiercely. 'No man worth his salt lays hands on a woman.'

Another gust of fat snowflakes blasted against them, coating men and horses.

'Well, I ain't riding out to the Lucky Dog in this weather for a half share of forty dollars,' McReadie answered. 'You act like some fool knight in armour iffen you wish; I'm turning back.' He reined his horse around and set off without waiting to see what the other man was doing.

Durrell dismounted, landing in fresh snow that was already four inches deep. He opened a saddle-bag, his hands clumsy with cold and the thick gloves, and took out a ball of grease wrapped in paper. Removing his right glove, he took a penknife from his pocket and began inspecting his horse's hoofs, clearing out the packed snow and smearing thick layers of grease into the sole of each foot. The grey stood with its head lowered, white snow settling in its white mane, as Jonah Durrell worked. By the time he finished, his right hand was red and stinging with cold. Durrell rapidly packed his things away, then pushed his right hand under the woollen saddle-blanket to warm it against his horse for a minute. McReadie was already out of sight by the time Jonah remounted and set off to find Spencer on his own.

★   ★   ★

The weather was crisp and bright the next morning, as Jonah Durrell rode up to the Lucky Dog mine. He took a moment to glance away from the drab, snow-covered mine buildings, to the sun-lit peaks of the mountains around him. Even after a couple of years living in Colorado, Jonah was still amazed by the clear air, and the way even the most distant, snow-glittering peaks were as clear to be seen as the nearest. Only the black smoke from the mine spoilt the purity of the landscape. The Lucky Dog was one of the few mines that kept working through the hard winter. The ore was dug and crushed, then stockpiled until the trails cleared enough for the trains of mules and burros to ship it south to Silverton. The mill itself was staggered in four storeys down the side of the mountain, a little way above the trail. An aerial tramway of ore cars connected it to the mine entrance, almost 500 feet higher up. The pounding of the stamp mills within the vast building was so loud Jonah could barely hear the hiss and rustle of snow as his horse walked.

Jonah had spent the night at the boarding-house of a smaller mine, four miles away. He had been thinking ahead, as usual. It had been dark when he'd arrived in the area, and there was no way he could return to Silverton with Spencer the same night. Neither did Jonah like the idea of spending the night guarding his prisoner before escorting him back in the morning. Instead, he chose to arrive at the Lucky Dog fresh, and unexpectedly, with a full day of travel ahead.

After leaving his horse in the warmth

of the stables, Jonah trudged through the snow to the two-storey boarding-house. He let himself in, finding himself in the main hall, and stopped to stamp the packed snow off his black boots. The air smelt warmly of coffee, beans and bacon as the men ate breakfast at long, wooden tables. Jonah's arrival caused a murmur of talk over the sounds of cutlery scraping tin plates. He ignored them for the moment, removing gloves, muffler and overcoat, hanging them from a peg on the wall. He automatically checked the set of his guns, and walked towards the tables, looking for Spencer.

There was a degree of envy in the way some of the men looked at him, for Jonah Durrell was an outstandingly handsome man. He stood a little over six foot tall, with broad shoulders and a slim waist. Black-haired and brown-eyed, he had a vivid presence and the gift of looking well-dressed in whatever he wore, though for preference, his clothes were of the finest quality. Jonah was disarmingly vain about his good looks, and fully aware of the different effects he had on men and women.

Jonah saw someone who matched the description he had, and moved around the tables, walking lightly and gracefully. Spencer had been described as having ears like a set of jug handles, and the brawny, fair man by the window certainly met that picture. Heads turned to watch and conversation died away as Jonah approached.

'Are you German Spencer?' Jonah asked, standing to one side of the seated man. The fair man swallowed a mouthful of beans and nodded. 'What do you want?'

'I'm taking you back to Silverton to face charges of assaulting Red Pearl,' Jonah answered calmly.

Spencer scowled. 'Damn whore wouldn't do like I wanted. She deserved it.'

Anger lit up Jonah's eyes. He had attended three years of medical college in New York before heading out West, and he'd been called in to see to the beaten woman's injuries. 'You beat her hard enough to crack her ribs and cause internal bleeding,' Jonah answered, his voice rising a little. 'Near on half her body was bruised.'

'A whore knows she's gonna get hit iffen she don't do like the man wants,' Spencer retorted. 'Hell, I'm payin' her; I kin do what I like with her, and it ain't no one else's business. So quit riding me and go back where you crawled from.' He spat a wad of brown saliva at the floor beside Jonah's boots, and turned back to the table. The crop-haired man sitting next to him laughed.

Jonah Durrell grabbed the grubby collar of Spencer's shirt and hauled him backwards, spilling him from his chair to the floor. He backed off a pace and waited for the cursing man to start rising. 'I'm taking you to Silverton,' he said firmly.

Spencer gathered his feet under himself and started to stand up. He was partway up when he suddenly lunged forward, aiming to headbutt Jonah in

8

the stomach. Jonah was expecting some such move, and side-stepped, hooking his leg between Spencer's to trip him up. Spencer sprawled onto the wooden floor for a second time.

Breakfast was forgotten as the other men watched the fight. Some miners climbed onto their table for a better view, yelling encouragement. Someone grabbed his tin coffee cup and started banging it on the table as he bellowed his support for Spencer. Spencer's crop-haired friend, Green, decided to show his support in a more practical way. As Jonah turned to face Spencer, Green seized Spencer's chair and threw it. The chair hit Jonah on the back, staggering him forwards. He caught his balance in time to meet Green, who was following up with a two-fisted attack. Jonah dodged one blow and knocked the other aside.

Spencer had regained his feet and was moving in to attack too. Thinking fast, Jonah stepped back a pace from Green, turned and swung into a high, powerful kick that caught Spencer in the stomach. Spencer gasped and folded onto his knees, clasping his stomach. Green closed in on Jonah, throwing wild, strong punches. Jonah turned again, dodged one and took the other on his shoulder. His thick winter clothing cushioned the impact. The two men faced one another and exchanged blows, with Jonah coming off best. Behind them, Spencer scrambled up again, cursing breathlessly. He was in pain, and bitterly aware of being humiliated in front of his friends. Glaring at Jonah, he drew the hunting knife he wore on his belt, and rushed forward.

'Look out!'

Jonah didn't know who was yelling, or who the warning was aimed at, but he heard the sudden clatter of boots behind him. He whirled around, his jacket flying open with the motion, and drew a gun, all in one smooth action. Spencer lunged, slashing the knife at Jonah's chest. Jonah twisted frantically, and fired at point-blank range as the knife tore into the shoulder of his jacket. Spencer gave a harsh cry, stumbling past and tumbling from the force of the shot. He landed face-down, the back of his shirt torn open and bloody.

Jonah switched the aim of his gun to Green. 'Don't move,' he commanded.

Green slowly wiped a smear of blood from his nose and raised his hands. His gaze flickered back and forth between Jonah and Spencer's body. A black-haired miner moved closer cautiously.

'Let me see him,' he requested, indicating Spencer, who wasn't moving.

'Go ahead.' Jonah studied Green's face for a moment, then reholstered his fancy revolver.

Green lowered his hands and watched with the gathering crowd as the black-haired miner and Jonah Durrell rolled Spencer's body over and examined it.

'Pretty near clean through the heart,' the miner commented. The cloth around the bullet wound was scorched and grained with gunpowder from the close shot.

'I'll pack him back to Silverton,' Jonah said, standing up.

No one made any objection. For one thing, the men had all seen the speed with which Jonah had drawn his gun, and also that he wore a matched pair. Fancy his Smith & Wessons might be, with pearl handles and engraved scrollwork, but they killed as well as a plain gun. Besides, not even Spencer's friend, Green, could deny Jonah's claim to have shot in self-defence.

Jonah Durrell glanced at the body on the floor, and remembered Red Pearl sobbing with pain, and Spencer's callous remarks. He wasn't sorry to see Spencer dead.

2

Motherlode looked and sounded much like every other town in the San Juans during the spring of 1876. The muddy streets rang to the sounds of hammering and sawing as new buildings were hastened up to cash in on the mining boom. Mining mills loomed on the slopes above the town; the people soon ceased to notice the non-stop rumble of heavy machinery as the precious ore was crushed for shipping. Jonah Durrell knew the sound of the stamp mills and welcomed it. The mills meant money, which bred greed and jealousy, which led to work for men like Jonah.

He guided his grey horse along the main street of Motherlode. Less than two years ago, this site had been a flat-bottomed, grassy valley caught between the towering canyon walls either side of the Animas River, as they closed together. Mule deer had roamed here, while beavers dammed sections of the braided river. Now the wild animals had moved on, the pines and aspen had been chopped down and fed into the sawmill, and a thriving town bestraddled the tumbling river.

This street, Panhandle Street, had the biggest and fanciest buildings in town. Most were genuine two-storeys, and a few, mostly the hotels and boarding-houses, were taller. Panhandle Street itself was busy. Jonah could see four wagons, two buckboards and a handful of other riders, but most noticeable were the burros and mules. Jonah reined in his horse to watch the fun, as twenty loaded burros being driven one way, met a train of two dozen mules being led the other. Burros were always driven loose in herds, not strung together. The mass of woolly animals merged with the mules, setting up a chorus of braying that even the stamp mills couldn't compete with. The muleskinner and the burro driver exchanged vehement curses as their animals milled together. Three mules promptly lay down in the street, while the rest tangled their ropes into a knot. Burros disappeared between the wooden buildings, their long ears flapping comically. Jonah's horse lay back its ears and snorted, apparently in distaste at the ill-manners of its relatives. Jonah gave up and burst out laughing.

He had recovered his composure by the time he reached the Marshal's office. This was a small, false-fronted building sandwiched between a haberdashery store and a restaurant. Two women leaving the haberdashery store looked at Jonah as he was dismounting, then looked again, longer. Jonah smiled at them and raised his hat, then sauntered into the marshal's office. Marshal Tapton looked up from his elderly copy of *The Police Gazette* as Jonah entered. Tapton was a work-toughened man, starting to spread at the waist as middle age set in. His craggy face was decorated with a flourishing moustache and side-whiskers, intended to draw attention from his impressive nose. Jonah immediately noticed the short-barrelled Civilian Colt the Marshal wore, and the shotguns and Winchesters racked neatly on the wall behind him. Marshal Tapton lowered his newspaper.

'Good afternoon,' Jonah said politely, unfastening his overcoat in the warmth of the overheated office.

The marshal looked him up and down, noting the red and gold brocade vest showing under Jonah's outer clothes and the other man's good looks. 'You'll be Jonah Durrell,' he said disapprovingly. The marshal's own clothes were plain and sober, and less expensive. 'You killed German Spencer a couple months back.'

'He came at me with a knife,' Jonah said simply.

Tapton grunted, accepting the defence. 'You looking for anyone here?'

'Not yet,' Jonah answered. 'I spent the winter in Silverton and took a fancy

16

to seeing somewhere new. I'd like to take a look at your wanted dodgers; catch up with what's happening round here.'

The marshal stood up and crossed the room to a converted wooden box that did service as a filing cabinet. 'What brought you out to Colorado?' he asked, rummaging in the box.

'I trailed up from Texas with an outfit bringing beef, two years ago.' Jonah perched himself on the edge of the desk as he talked. 'I liked the country so I stayed on, hunting game at first, to sell to miners. When more people started coming into the area, I found it paid better to hunt men.'

Marshal Tapton handed him a sheaf of papers. 'You don't talk like you're from Texas.'

'Vermont,' Jonah answered, scanning the top sheet of paper. 'My father's a doctor, and I studied three years at medical college. I couldn't stick any more lectures and dissecting things, so I quit and went to Texas.'

'So now you shoot folks, instead of healing them.'

Jonah looked up. 'I can do some doctor work when I need to. I kept my instruments; I can stitch wounds, set bones and deliver babies. And the only men I shoot are the ones the law gives me the right to shoot.'

'The power of life and death in one man,' the marshal said reflectively. 'That's a heap of power for one man.'

'It's a living,' Jonah said flippantly, his attention on the wanted dodgers. He skimmed through all the sheets, laying half a dozen aside. Those he picked up again and read in more detail.

Marshal Tapton picked up his copy of *The Police Gazette* and leaned against the wall, unwilling to sit in the chair at his desk while Jonah was still sitting on the desk. The marshal rustled and fluffed his paper into shape, and slowly read a short article. Jonah took no notice, his attention now wholly devoted to the wanted papers. He considered each thoroughly before setting one aside.

'What do you know about this Goff?' he asked, taking a small notepad and silver pencil from the pocket of his fancy waistcoat. He started copying information from the wanted poster.

Tapton lowered his paper and thought for a moment. 'That's the feller killed a gambler a couple of months back, right?' Jonah grunted agreement. Tapton continued, 'It happened in the Ginger Cat. Seems like the tinhorn, Jacobi, reckoned that Goff had welshed on his bet. Goff reckoned Jacobi was working with a stacked deck. It wound up with Goff shooting Jacobi and hightailing out of town, and out of my jurisdiction.'

Jonah nodded; he'd seen and heard such things himself. 'Was Goff known around Motherlode?'

'Yes. He came in last year when the town was plotted and the first buildings went up. Seemed to have some experience of prospecting. Came into town now and again for supplies.'

Jonah finished copying the information he wanted and put the notebook and pencil away.

'Reckon I might go take a look for Goff,' he remarked.

The marshal nodded, though there was little enthusiasm in his expression.

'Anything else you want to know?' he asked.

Jonah smiled. 'Can you tell me the names of the best hotel in town, the best barber, and the best brothel, please?'

★   ★   ★

It was dark when Jonah Durrell rapped the well-polished brass door-knocker and waited outside Miss Jenny's house. Curtains had been drawn in the windows of the large, well-built house, but one pair had been left just far enough apart to display a lamp with a fancy, red glass shade. Jonah stroked his jaw as he waited, pleased with the smoothness of the shave. The marshal's recommendations for hotel and barber had been good, so Jonah was feeling optimistic about Miss Jenny's parlour-house.

The door was opened by a smartly-dressed black man named Albert, who studied Jonah for a moment before ushering him inside. The mingled smells of perfume, furniture polish and good food greeted Jonah as he entered. The hall had papered walls, decorated with tasteful silhouette pictures of female heads. A small, mahogany table held a vase with a bright display of wild spring flowers. Feminine voices and laughter carried to him from the two rooms that opened off the hall, vying with the music of a piano. The air of comfort and companionship brought a smile to Jonah's face just as Miss Jenny appeared.

'Good evening,' she said, smiling as Jonah bowed politely to her. 'Welcome to my boarding-house.'

Good manners kept Jonah from showing his surprise at his first sight of the madam. Miss Jenny was the tallest woman he'd ever seen, at least as tall as himself. The long skirt of her elegant grey dress made it impossible to tell how high the heels of her shoes were, but Jonah guessed her to be about six foot tall. Glossy dark hair piled high added to the impression of height. Miss Jenny carried herself well, comfortable with her height. She had merry, dark eyes, that sparkled from beneath a fringe of the glossy hair, and a bright smile that Jonah warmed to at once. He guessed her to be in her late twenties, young for a parlour-house madam.

'My name is Jonah Durrell.' He introduced himself as he unfastened his coat. 'Marshal Tapton recommended your establishment.' Jonah knew that high-class parlour-houses often required references or letters of introduction from new clients. As Jenny nodded, he took off his coat and hat, handing them to the modestly dressed young maid who had been waiting in the background.

'The marshal disapproves of this form of business,' Jenny remarked evenly. 'But so long as we pay our taxes and buy a licence, he leaves us alone.' She paused, and studied Jonah's gunbelt.

'I'd rather keep these with me,' Jonah said, brushing one gun butt with his hand. 'I'm not expecting any trouble, but in my profession, it's as well to be prepared.'

Miss Jenny nodded and then smiled. 'Let me introduce you to some of my boarders.'

Jonah followed her through an archway into the room on the right of the hall. The papered walls here were decorated with paintings of nearly-nude women, but Jonah preferred to look at the live ones in front of him. All were lovely, and finely dressed in silk, satin and velvet. Jonah's spirits rose at the sight of them, the sound of their voices, the rustling of the fine fabrics as they moved, and the scent of perfume. Jonah loved the company of women. He liked them as friends, he enjoyed their appreciation of his good looks, and he looked at them with pleasure in return.

Miss Jenny introduced him to the six young women present and after a few minutes chatting to them, Jonah asked Miss Erica to have dinner with him. He offered her his arm, and took her through to the dining-room.

'I couldn't resist your English accent,' he told her as they sat at one of the linen-covered tables. 'I guess you must find things rather different out here in the West.'

Miss Erica smiled back at him. 'I certainly do. But a lot of them are very welcome differences.'

Before meeting Miss Jenny, Jonah would have described Miss Erica as being tall for a woman. Erica was a classical English beauty with a clear, creamy complexion and blue eyes that shone with a love of life. Her dark brown, wavy hair was taken up at the sides but the rest tumbled down her back, almost to her hips.

'What kind of differences?' Jonah prompted.

'I like the western saddles, and I love

riding astride,' Erica answered enthusiastically. 'I'd never dare do that back home. If I arrived at a meet riding astride, everyone would think the world was about to end!' She looked astonished at the thought of her own audacity.

Jonah laughed along with her. 'Do you go riding regularly?'

'Most days,' Erica replied. 'Miss Jenny, Helen, Megan and I all have horses. I love to get out into the fresh air and have a good gallop.'

'The air here in Colorado is like nowhere else I've ever been,' Jonah said. 'So remarkably clear and pure.'

They talked easily throughout the excellent meal. During dessert, the chat turned more flirtatious. Miss Erica's eyes sparkled mischievously as she smiled and joked. She leaned forward as she spoke, giving Jonah a fine view of her cleavage; soft, peachy breasts framed in the lace trim of her low-cut blue dress. He reached across the table, capturing her hand in his left hand, and gently stroking the palm with the fingertips of his right hand. Erica made a soft sound of surprise and pleasure.

'I've had enough to eat,' Jonah said quietly. 'I reckon I'm ready for bed.'

'Shall we go upstairs?'

In expensive parlour-houses like Miss Jenny's, everything was done to keep up the illusion that the business was not, in fact, a business. The bar in one parlour, the piano in the other, and the dining-room provided time for pleasant social exchange with the girls. As Jonah and Erica left the dining-room, they met Miss Jenny in the hall.

'Was the meal satisfactory?' she asked.

'It was excellent,' Jonah answered, taking out his wallet. 'As is the company.' He handed his money directly to Jenny. It was all part of the routine, making-believe that the pay-ment was for the meal, not for the services of the lovely woman at his side. A cynical part of Jonah knew that making payment direct to the madam also ensured that the girls didn't have the chance to keep back any part of their fee.

Once in the comfortable privacy of Erica's well-appointed room, Jonah gently clasped his hands behind her neck and drew her close for a kiss. She responded warmly before breaking off to unfasten the mother-of-pearl buttons on his brocade waistcoat. 'You are very handsome,' she remarked. 'And you dress well. I bet you're vain.' Her voice was teasing as she slowly undid the buttons.

'I'm as vain as the day is long,' Jonah answered cheerfully, unfastening his gunbelt to hang it over the footboard of the bed. 'And then after dark, as well.'

'I hate vain men.' She slid the waistcoat off and draped it over the bedpost.

Jonah curled his arms around her waist and started unfastening her elaborate skirts. 'In that case, you must hate me.'

'Oh, I do.' Erica unfastened her

hoops while he hung the skirts neatly over a frame. She moved behind him and kissed the back of his neck before sliding his braces over his shoulders.

Jonah let her unfasten his trousers and managed to step out of them elegantly as she slid them down his legs. 'It's a shame that I intend to have my wicked way with you then.' He gave her a melodramatic leer.

Erica held up her hands in mock distress. 'Oh! Oh! Won't somebody help me?' She spoke far too quietly to be heard outside the room.

Jonah started unfastening the tiny buttons down the front of her bodice. 'There's no point in crying for help,' he warned. 'I have you in my evil clutches now.'

Erica nearly broke out giggling, but managed to control herself. She let Jonah slide her bodice off, and started unfastening his silk shirt in return. 'I don't think I've ever been ravished by a villain before,' she said.

'The villains are always more interesting, and I'm rotten to the core.' Jonah kissed her again.

Erica slid her hands across his broad chest as she peeled his shirt off. 'Oh, yes, you're a thoroughly bad apple.'

Jonah stood back and flexed his muscles in the manner of a circus strongman. He was clad only in his long underpants; Erica still wore her corset, a silk chemise and lace-edged drawers. She still had the air of a born lady, in spite of her undress, and the mischief in her lovely face.

'You look like an advertisement for an iron tonic,' she said, smothering giggles.

'I'm not an advertisement, I'm the real item,' he boasted, humour gleaming in his eyes. 'And I can prove it too.' Moving swiftly, he embraced Erica and kissed her passionately. They were just drawing apart when a woman screamed.

3

It was a scream of complete and utter terror, and ended with a horrible abruptness. Durrell and Erica froze, looking into one another's eyes. The sound had come from a room about halfway down the corridor. Durrell was the first to recover. He snatched his gunbelt off the bedpost and hurtled into the corridor. Other doors were opening as he ran in the direction the sound had come from.

'That was Lucy,' another girl called, pointing to the room next to her own.

Erica was right behind Durrell as he stopped outside the solid wooden door. He drew one revolver and thrust the gunbelt at her. He cocked the revolver and stood alongside the wall to try the door. It wasn't locked, so he shoved it wide open and dashed inside. The room was lit by a single lamp but there was enough light for Jonah to see one figure lying among tangled bedclothes, and the curtains blowing beside the open window. He raced to the bed and bent over to see Lucy gasping frantically as scarlet blood bubbled from her nose and mouth. More blood poured from the gaping wound ripped across her neck. The pillows and sheets were already saturated as Jonah knelt briefly beside her.

'Who was it?' he demanded.

Lucy turned her eyes towards him but when she tried to speak, blood bubbled from her mouth and gargled in her throat. Erica was beside the bed too, leaning over the dying woman.

'Comfort her,' Jonah ordered, rising. He sprinted to the window and looked down into the alley beside the building. Clasping the barrel of his revolver between his teeth, he climbed onto the windowsill, let himself down by his arms, and dropped the last few feet onto the dirt surface.

Jonah quickly recovered his balance

and stooped to look for tracks. There was little light, but the ground was soft enough to show him that whoever had jumped from the window before him had run into Panhandle Street. Jonah sprinted that way too, his gun ready. As he reached the end of the alley, he glimpsed movement to his left, by the corner of the Shovel saloon. A man was running fast, his pale shirt showing up in the darkness. Jonah came to a halt, shouting across the wide street as he raised his gun.

'Halt, or I'll shoot!'

The running man kept going without looking back. Jonah fired one shot, but his suspect disappeared around the corner of the saloon uninjured. Jonah gave chase, running diagonally across the street. The Shovel was on the corner of Panhandle Street and a short street that ended in a footbridge. By the time Jonah reached the corner, there was no one in sight. If the man he had been chasing had crossed the wooden bridge, he could be anywhere among the cluster of shanties on the other side of the Animas River. Jonah didn't know the layout of that part of town, and didn't fancy the risk of walking into an ambush. He had one gun, and no reloads, and suddenly realized he was wearing nothing but his long underpants.

'Son-of-a-bitch,' he muttered to himself.

Jonah turned around to head back to the brothel. As he crossed the street, a bunch of miners spilled from the door of the saloon. A chorus of catcalls and whistles arose as they saw Jonah, half-naked and spattered to the knees with dirt. For once, Jonah's sense of humour deserted him. He spun around and fired a single shot into the nameboard of the saloon, over the rowdy miners' heads. They abruptly fell silent. Jonah turned his back on them and stalked back to Miss Jenny's house.

★ ★ ★

By the time Jonah had washed the dirt off his feet and got dressed again,

Marshal Tapton had arrived and looked at Miss Lucy's body. The parlour-house seemed a different place now. There was no music from the piano, no laughter, or the light chatter of female voices. The girls were gathered together in the parlour, some sobbing, and comforting one another. As Jonah entered the parlour, Miss Erica handed him a flower-patterned china cup, filled with black coffee. He took it gratefully, and inhaled the warm aroma as he looked around the room.

There were some girls present Jonah hadn't seen before. One was rather strikingly different, for although as well dressed as the others, she was short and overflowingly plump. Her round, blue eyes were thoughtful as she hugged a slender young woman with a long fall of thick, golden hair. Marshal Tapton's plain black clothes struck a sober note amongst the brighter colours, lace and frills of the women's clothing. The marshal beckoned Jonah over to join himself and Miss Jenny by the window.

'I hear tell you lost track of the feller on the other side of the footbridge?' Tapton drawled, pulling at the ends of his long moustache.

'That's so,' Jonah agreed. He gave the marshal a clear and straightforward account of what he had done, from the time of hearing Lucy's scream, to his return to the parlour-house. 'I doubt if I'd recognize the killer if I saw him again in daylight,' Jonah commented. He looked at Jenny, noticing that the light had gone from her dark eyes. 'Do you know anything about him?'

'He said his name was Tom Halesworth,' Jenny answered. 'He was wearing a cheap, ready-made brown suit, but his boots were better quality. He was clean and fresh-shaved: clean-shaved. I thought he wasn't used to visiting fancy places, but he had the money and was making the effort to act like he thought a gentleman would, so I decided to take his business.' Jenny closed her eyes for a moment, controlling her feelings.

Jonah reached out and gently touched

her arm. 'You couldn't have guessed what he intended to do.'

She looked at him and smiled her thanks for his sympathy.

'Did he have a gun on him when he arrived?' Marshal Tapton asked.

Jenny shook her head. 'Nothing I could see, though he may have had a derringer hidden somewhere.'

'What was his voice like?' Jonah asked. 'Did he have a distinct accent?' This time Miss Jenny paused to think before she answered. 'No real accent I could pinpoint. Not southern, or New England, or foreign. Not well-educated, anyway.' She shook her head in frustration. 'He was remarkably ordinary.'

'Ideal attribute for someone who doesn't want to be noticed or remembered,' Jonah remarked. He turned to the marshal. 'If you want my help at all, just ask.'

Marshal Tapton tugged the end of his moustache. 'Thanks, but he's probably headed for tall timber by now. I'll ask around, but I don't reckon there's much chance of finding this Halesworth.'

'Halesworth just murdered a woman,' Jonah retorted, his voice beginning to rise along with his temper.

Tapton was unperturbed. 'Whores know the risk they take when they start selling their bodies.'

The quiet conversations in the room died away. Jenny's face became bright with anger as she faced the marshal.

'You don't know the first thing about women like Lucy,' she snapped. 'She was a sweet girl who never harmed anyone in her life. She did nothing to deserve getting killed like that.'

'She lived her life in sin,' Tapton answered. 'And she paid for that sin.'

'For some women, it's a choice between sinning, and starving,' Jenny told him plainly. 'Can you blame them for choosing not to starve?'

Marshal Tapton glanced around the room, seeing the well-dressed, well-fed women of Jenny's parlour-house staring at him with expressions ranging from guilt to anger. He sighed gustily, setting the ends of his moustache fluttering. A look at Jonah showed him a man clearly on the edge of losing his temper. Tapton shrugged, losing nothing of his heavy self-possession.

'I said I'll look into it,' he repeated, and turned to leave.

Jonah occupied himself for a few moments with his coffee, letting his anger cool down before he spoke. As the marshal was shown out by Albert, the women's voices rose again. Jonah overheard Miss Erica stating that if she could find whoever had killed Miss Lucy, she would happily empty both barrels of her shotgun into him. He caught Jenny's eye, and raised a half-smile for her.

'I reckon you were about right when you said the marshal disapproved of your business,' he said.

'No men ever care about what happens to prostitutes,' Jenny answered bitterly.

'Some do,' Jonah answered fiercely. 'I could have pounded that marshal into the ground when he talked about Lucy paying for her sins. The world is never so simple as his sort like to make out, and no lawman worthy of the title should let a man get away with killing a woman. If Marshal Tapton won't make an effort to find this Halesworth, I damn well shall.'

Jonah was too absorbed with his own feelings to notice the spark of hope that slowly warmed Miss Jenny's eyes.

★   ★   ★

Miss Jenny was the last one to get to bed that night, and one of the first up the next morning. She chose a simple, grey day-dress and had her young maid arrange her hair in a neat coiled braid.

'I shall have to go fix up Lucy's funeral,' Jenny explained to her maid. 'I think Middleton's Hardware Emporium has some coffins in stock, and

39

we'll need to arrange for a wagon to do as a hearse.'

'Do you think that man will come back?' Lizzie, the maid, asked anxiously. Jenny mustered a reassuring smile. 'I really don't think so. Albert and I both had a good look at him. He knows that either of us could identify him if we saw him again, and I bet some of the girls who were working last night would remember him too.' Jenny was pleased to see Lizzie, who was just sixteen, relax and smile too.

Before Miss Jenny could leave to make the arrangements for the funeral, she had an unexpected visitor. He introduced himself as Adam Sharpe, the owner of the Silver Lode saloon, further down Panhandle Street.

'I heard about what happened last night, and I wanted to offer my condolences,' he said, sweeping off a wide-brimmed black hat that was decorated with silver conchos.

Jenny invited him to sit down with

her in the music parlour, and offered coffee.

'Thank you,' Sharpe settled himself in an armchair and looked around. 'I'm just sorry I didn't call on you in more pleasant circumstances. It must have been a horrible shock to you all.'

'It was very frightening,' Jenny admitted. She studied Adam Sharpe as he gazed at the lavish parlour furnishings.

He was reasonably tall, though some four inches shorter than she was herself. Having been born and raised in a brothel, eventually working as a prostitute, then as a madam, Jenny was very quick at assessing details about men. She guessed, correctly, that Sharpe was in his late 30s. His dark hair was noticeably silvered at the temples, but with his clean-cut, slightly aquiline features, Sharpe looked distinguished. He had an air of confidence that was reflected in the good quality of his clothes. Sharpe favoured the style of a gambler, and wore a grey, cut-away coat over a frilly-fronted shirt with a black, bootlace tie. Jenny noticed both the Colt revolver he wore in a well-made black holster, and the silver ring on the little finger of his right hand.

'If the girl who died was as charming as you, Miss Jenny, her death will be a loss to those who knew her.' Sharpe smiled warmly at her.

One of the parlour maids came in with cups of coffee on a tray. She set the tray on a small table between their chairs and left as quietly as she had entered, leaving Jenny to serve her visitor. When cream and sugar had been added, and the hot coffee sampled, Sharpe took up the conversation again.

'Is the marshal hopeful of catching the murderer?'

Jenny shook her head. 'I don't think Marshal Tapton's like to catch anyone unless the killer walks into his office and makes a full confession.' Anger spilled into her voice. 'The marshal reckons that getting slaughtered like a stuck pig is just routine for whores. He doesn't see any reason to get bothered about it.'

Sharpe shook his head. 'That's a for-real shame. These mining towns are woolly places, sure enough, and if you can't rely on the law to protect folks, no-one's likely to sleep safe in their beds.'

Jenny sipped her coffee and let out a short sigh. 'Most of my girls are holding up pretty well, but Linda was talking about packing up and heading back to New Orleans.'

'She might be wise,' Sharpe said. 'If your girls don't feel safe here, or move away, your business could run into trouble.' He glanced again at the papered walls, the carved bar, and the well-made furniture as he drank his coffee. 'You could stand to lose a lot of money,' he said sympathetically.

Jenny understood very well the validity of his remark. To set up a top-class parlour-house like this meant a high initial outlay. Not only was there the cost of the fittings and furnishings, but also the additional expense of having them transported out to such a remote, mountainous area. Jenny knew how quickly a mining town could boom and bust, and had thought long and hard before choosing Motherlode to set up business.

'I won't pull out in a hurry,' she told Sharpe.

'Of course not,' Sharpe agreed, smiling warmly at her. 'You got sense and you've got guts, I'm sure of that.' Jenny started to smile back as he went on, 'But I'm sure you've got sense enough to know when to quit. And if the law won't look after you, and you paying your licence fee and all, then maybe you'd best keep an open mind.'

Jenny occupied herself for a moment with her coffee. 'Whoever that man was, Halesworth, he called himself, he won't come back here, I'm sure of that. He'd be recognized as soon as he put his face anywhere near the door. I've seen girls get beaten up, half-strangled; all kinds of trouble. That's why I'd rather put my money into one good parlour-house than run a couple of cheap cat houses. I don't get the drunken fools out to blow their last two bucks on a bit of quick relief. I care about my girls,' she added passionately.

Sharpe nodded, putting his hand gently on her arm. 'That's plain enough to see. Now, Miss Jenny, you know you can call on me at the Silver Lode, anytime you need help. I don't reckon the marshal cares for saloon folk much more than he cares about you and your girls. So we've got to stick together and that way we'll pull through.'

'Thank you.' Jenny's face brightened.

Adam Sharpe stood up and turned to face her. 'You know, if there's too much trouble here, I'd make you a good offer for this place.'

Jenny barely had to think before shaking her head. 'That's kind of you, but I doubt if I'm going to sell out.'

Sharpe took her hand and helped Jenny from her chair. He kept hold of her hand for a moment longer than necessary and gave it a quick squeeze before releasing it. 'It's always a pleasure to help out a lovely lady.'

Jenny accepted the compliment with an automatic smile. Sharpe's flirting was well done but there seemed to be something missing from his eyes when he looked at her.

As they entered the hall, Albert opened the door to let in Jonah Durrell. Jenny's face lit up with a wide, genuine smile as she saw the handsome man.

'Good morning, Miss Jenny,' he greeted her respectfully. 'How are you this morning?'

'I've had better days, Jonah.' Jenny took his hand and held it for a few moments, smiling at him, before turning her attention to her other guest.

There was no warmth in Adam Sharpe's eyes as he studied Jonah Durrell. Jonah was a little taller than he was, ten years younger, equally well dressed and so confidently handsome.

She introduced the two men, without mentioning Jonah's occupation. 'Jonah was here last night when Lucy was murdered,' she told Sharpe. 'He chased the killer but lost him over the footbridge.'

'I sure wish I'd been able to get some lead into that son-of-a-bitch,' Jonah said.

'That's a fine pair of irons you're wearing,' Sharpe commented, looking at Jonah's matched Smith & Wessons.

'Tools of the trade,' Jonah answered.

Adam Sharpe raised an eyebrow. 'Inside or outside the law?'

Jonah was unworried by the comment. 'I'm a manhunter,' he said straightforwardly. 'I see that the law catches up with those who need it. I'm good at my job,' he added, a hint of pride and challenge in his eyes.

'It's a plumb shame that whoever killed that girl last night got away from you,' Sharpe said. 'Still, it was mighty good of you to chase after him.'

'Any man would have done the same,' Jonah answered.

'I can think of at least one marshal who wouldn't,' Jenny remarked.

Jonah nodded and amended his

remark. 'Any man *should* have done the same.' He took Jenny's arm a moment. 'Will you let me know when you've got Lucy's funeral fixed up. I'd like to attend.'

'That's very kind of you,' Jenny answered softly. 'I'll do that.'

Adam Sharpe spoke up. 'In the meantime, how about coming along to the Silver Lode this evening, Durrell? I reckon your gallantry deserves a free drink or two.'

Jonah considered the offer for a moment. 'I think I will; thank you.' He turned to Miss Jenny and smiled at her once more. 'I'll leave you to get on. And don't forget to come ask if you need anything I can help with.'

'I'll be going, too,' Sharpe said, taking Jenny's hand. 'Don't forget what I said earlier.' He squeezed her hand briefly and smiled.

The two men left together, leaving Miss Jenny to think about their overlapping visits. She thought about Jonah Durrell for rather longer than Adam Sharpe.

4

The door to Adam Sharpe's private office at the back of the Silver Lode was firmly closed, but the sound of miners singing along with the entertainer on stage was still audible. There was little risk though, of the conversation inside the room being overheard outside. Sharpe was sitting at his desk, cradling a glass of whiskey between his hands as he described Jonah Durrell to the man standing on the other side of the desk. The other man, Barker, listened and stayed quiet until Sharpe finished speaking.

'I heard tell as how Jonah Durrell is pretty handy with his irons,' Barker remarked, looking steadily at his boss. Barker was an unmemorable man, noticeable only for his powerful chest and arms and a vast moustache that usually had a few crumbs caught in it.

49

He wore a plain Colt in an ordinary, slightly scuffed, brown holster.

'I don't want you to get into a shooting match with him,' Sharpe said. 'I just want to see some bruises on that handsome face. He won't go round smirking at women after he's had his nose flattened across his face.' Sharpe heard the jealousy creeping into his voice and managed to keep his tone more neutral. He lifted the whiskey glass and swallowed some of the amber liquid.

Barker affected a bland look. 'Does he have any friends like to take his side?'

'Durrell only arrived in town yesterday,' Sharpe reassured him. 'Marshal Tapton said he'd never been here before.' After leaving Jenny's parlour-house, Sharpe had made it his business to learn more about Jonah Durrell's business.

Barker nodded and gave a grunt of satisfaction. 'I'll be ready for him.'

Sharpe smiled and raised his glass in salute.

Jonah Durrell's spirits rose as he entered the noisy, lively saloon midway through the evening. He was content with his own company when riding after wanted men but he thrived best in the company of others. The click and rattle of the gambling games, the smells of liquor, bodies and beer, the buzz of voices and laughter all brought a smile to his face as he made his way to the long bar. It seemed that like Miss Jenny, Adam Sharpe was also determined to make a go of business in Motherlode. The Silver Lode was a large, well-set-up saloon, with a stage at the back where a row of girls danced with more energy than grace. The paint on the lumber walls and ceiling had already taken on the yellowed tint of nicotine. Behind the bar was a long mirror, which reflected light from the oil lamps back into the smoky room.

Jonah couldn't see the saloon owner among the crowds, so ordered himself a glass of good whiskey and took it to a small table not far from the stage. He enjoyed watching the dancing, but it wasn't long before one of the floor girls appeared beside him.

'You look kind of lonesome,' she remarked, smiling.

Jonah liked her smile, and her pretty, heart-shaped face, so he invited her to sit down and introduced himself.

'I'm Maybelline,' she replied, settling her knee-length skirts with a delicious rustling of petticoats. 'You're new in town, ain't you? I'd sure remember iffen I'd done seen you around before,' she added warmly.

'And I'm sure I'd remember that beauty spot,' Jonah answered, pointing to a mole just above her left breast. It showed up particularly well on her fair skin.

Maybelline giggled, which had the entrancing effect of making the beauty spot jiggle. Jonah ordered a glass of wine for her and they soon fell into cheerful conversation.

The pleasant evening was abruptly interrupted by a voice snarling at Jonah.

'The woman was keeping me company.'

Jonah looked up and saw a strongly-built man whose large moustache was damp with beer, and decorated with a couple of unidentifiable crumbs.

'The lady was unaccompanied when she approached me,' he replied, emphasizing the word 'lady'.

Barker snorted. 'I never saw no *lady* wear a dress cut so low you kin see half her apples.'

Maybelline instinctively covered the neckline of her dress with one hand.

Jonah felt his temper rising, and spoke boldly. 'It's not so hard to guess why she didn't want any more of your company. I never yet met a woman who preferred to keep the company of hogs. Someone should get you a yard broom to clean out that moustache for a start.'

Barker's face flushed. He'd picked this fight because Sharpe had told him to, but he was going to thoroughly enjoy pummeling that handsome, dandy-dressed manhunter.

'Maybe she likes things dirty 'cause she's a dirty whore herself,' he answered, leering at Maybelline.

Jonah exploded up out of his chair, his fist going straight for Barker's face. His speed surprised Barker, who jerked backwards barely fast enough to avoid the worst of the blow. Barker staggered backwards, colliding with another man who cursed as his beer slopped from his glass. Jonah Durrell stood straight, fists raised.

'You apologize now,' he ordered Barker.

Barker's reply was a brief obscenity, followed by a double-handed attack.

Maybelline and other people around scattered hurriedly as the two men began to fight in earnest. Jonah had a slight advantage of reach on Barker, but couldn't match him for sheer power. He soon realized that Barker was a better-than-average fist fighter, and that the other man was determined to leave his mark on Jonah's face. Barker waded in with a series of heavy punches, forcing Jonah to go on the defensive. Jonah kept his hands high, occasionally retaliating with a quick blow to the side of Barker's solid head. Advice was being yelled from all directions as the fight developed. As he ducked around, Jonah got a few glimpses of the girls on the stage, still dancing and kicking their legs higher in an effort to keep the audience's attention, and stop them from getting involved in the fight.

'Whyn't you start fightin' back?' Barker taunted, swinging a hefty punch that Jonah deflected. 'You afraid of getting yer nose flattened across that dime-novel hero face of your'n?' He was breathing deep and fast, his eyes shining with delight in his own prowess.

'You're hardly the first one to want to break my nose,' Jonah answered, circling to his right. 'No one's succeeded yet. Look!' On the last word, he moved his hands away from his face and grinned at his opponent.

Barker was too startled to react right away, then jerked back his right fist, ready to punch Jonah full in the face. Jonah had already started moving. He stepped quickly to his left and rammed both fists hard into Barker's belly. Barker gasped, losing his wind, and put his own fists up as he started to back away. Jonah followed in fast, striking a blow into Barker's gut that bent him over, then swung a round punch with the other hand, landing on Barker's left eye. The skin around Barker's eye split, leaving a smear of blood on Jonah's knuckles.

Barker jabbed upwards, catching the side of Jonah's jaw, but there wasn't much power in it. Jonah was thinking fast, as he always did. He was new in town, an unknown quantity. There would most likely be other men who would resent his looks, his money, or even his educated speech. Another time he would have been willing to give Barker a chance to surrender. Now though, he could use Barker as an example. Jonah brushed Barker's arm aside and lunged in with a beautiful uppercut to Barker's jaw. Barker grunted and staggered backwards. He hit the edge of a table, lost his balance and fell heavily onto his backside.

Jonah went after him, motivated by practical reasons rather than revenge. A reputation as a tough fighter was a useful tool for a manhunter. Jonah closed fast and lashed out with a kick, that hit Barker high up on the chest. It wasn't as vicious as a kick to the head would have been, but it was plenty powerful enough to lay Barker flat out on the floor, groaning. Jonah looked down at him for a moment, then turned away, smoothing down his hair and straightening his clothes.

He saw Sharpe just as the saloon owner hailed him.

'My, I'm real sorry that happened,' the saloon owner exclaimed, taking Durrell's arm. He peered into the other man's face. 'No damage done, I sure hope?'

'Just some bruises,' Jonah answered cheerfully. 'Nothing time won't cure.'

He was too busy adjusting the set of his jacket to notice the venomous look that flashed across Sharpe's face.

Sharpe rapidly recovered himself, and led Durrell to the bar. 'I promised you a drink, and you'll be wanting a slug of something now.'

Jonah nodded. 'I could use something to clean the taste of that cur's words away.'

'I'll tell the staff to keep an eye on him.' Sharpe promised. 'He'll learn to hold his tongue in the future.'

'I can't stand to hear a man badmouthing a woman,' Jonah said sincerely.

Adam Sharpe nodded, and mentally filed the comment away for later use. For now, he was willing to bide his time, but sooner or later, Jonah Durrell was going to get his handsome face rubbed in the dirt.

★   ★   ★

The next morning, men and women going about their business in the streets of Motherlode paused to watch Miss Lucy's cortège pass by. The infant town could boast of five saloons, three brothels and a pool hall, but there was no church or ordained minister to speak for the young woman as she went to her final resting place. Her plain pine coffin rode in the back of a borrowed wagon, driven by Albert, doorman of the parlour-house. Jenny, her girls, the maids and the parlour-house cook all walked behind the wagon as it rumbled along Panhandle Street and turned into Puddle Street. All were soberly dressed, managing at least a token of black in their clothing. After the parlour-house folk came the few other mourners, Jonah Durrell and Adam Sharpe amongst them.

On Puddle Street, they passed the two other brothels. At both the Black Cat, and then again at the Velvet Cushion, the madam and her girls came and stood outside as the funeral passed. A few of the girls silently joined the mourners and walked with them as they passed between Dawson's Freight and the sad row of cribs at the edge of town. The horses leaned into their collars as they hauled the wagon up the trail to the sloping burial ground above the town.

There, Miss Lucy's coffin was lowered into her grave, one of a bare half-dozen there.

A few words were spoken in memory of the murdered woman, then Jonah stepped forward, as Jenny had asked earlier, to deliver the Lord's Prayer. His clear voice carried well to those around the grave:

'Our Father, who art in heaven, hallowed be thy Name . . . '

It was the only prayer publicly spoken for Miss Lucy.

* * *

That afternoon, Jonah Durrell visited Motherlode's land office. The one-storey lumber building was tucked between the Shovel Saloon, and the cold tumbling waters of the Animas

River. Jonah paused outside the Land Office, looking at the footbridge that spanned the river there, and the half-dozen shanty homes on the other side. This was where he had lost track of Lucy's murderer. Beyond the shanties, the ground rose sharply. Scrubby grass covered the thin soil lower down, with the bare, red bones of rock poking through. Higher, the massed ranks of pine carpeted the mountain, liberally dressed with snow that would linger for another couple of months yet. Though the view was beautiful, it was not peaceful. Mine buildings perched on the lower slopes, the stamps pounding and smoke pouring from chimneys into the blue sky. A path had been slashed through the trees for an aerial tramway that connected the mine itself to the processing buildings. Jonah wondered how the miners who lived in the adjacent boarding-house ever got any rest. He took a deep breath of the clear, exhilarating air, and opened the door into the pleasant warmth of the office.

The agent, Richard Jeapes, was at his carefully organized desk, busy copying documents. He gestured for Jonah to sit down, and immediately bent over his work again. Jonah unfastened his heavy overcoat and settled into the wooden chair. His attention was drawn to the large map of the Red Mountain fixed to the wall; he studied it with professional interest as the pen-nib scratched across the paper.

After a few minutes, the agent wiped his pen, put it back in its holder, and neatly blotted his work, lining the thick blotting paper precisely over the close lines of copper-plate writing. The document was inspected one more time, then set carefully aside.

'Most sorry to have kept you waiting,' Jeapes said. 'How may I help?'

'Jonah Durrell.' Jonah watched the other man's face as he spoke, searching for any sign of reaction. The agent looked thoughtful, as though trying to place the name. 'I'm looking for someone who's taken off into the mountains. I want to find out if he's got a claim registered around here; that's most likely where he's at.'

Jeapes's expression cleared. 'You're a manhunter, aren't you? I heard tell you got mixed up with that business of the parlour-house girl being murdered.'

Jonah nodded. 'I was at Miss Jenny's place when it happened.'

The agent studied him with greater interest. 'Is that the feller you're looking for?'

'Not right now,' Jonah answered. 'Though I'd sure like to find the son-of-a-bitch that slaughtered Miss Lucy. The man I'm here about shot a gambler. I'm looking for Goff.'

'I remember something about that,' Jeapes commented, getting up to look in one of his filing cabinets. 'He got into an argument with the tinhorn. Got a temper like a rattler poked with a stick, if I recollect right.' He pulled out a cardboard folder, glanced at the contents, then laid it on the desk in front of Jonah. 'There you go. Goff.'

5

Jonah left the Land Office with the information he wanted. He knew where Goff's claim was, but he couldn't see any point in heading off there at that time of day. There was little chance of getting into the mountains and back before dark now. Jonah saw no reason to spend the night camped in the snowy mountains if he didn't have to. He decided to take a good look around Motherlode. It was a habit to get to know the layout of a town whenever possible. Knowing where the shortcuts were, and which alleys were dead-ends, could make a real difference to a man's chances.

Turning right along Panhandle Street, Jonah passed the bank, a café and the marshal's office. Jonah frowned at the sight of the marshal's office, thinking of the law man's indifference to the fate of

Miss Lucy. The thought of what he'd like to say to the marshal on the subject occupied him as he passed the plain lumber building. He was jogged suddenly from his thoughts as he passed the next building, and caught a glimpse of movement from the corner of his eye. A moment later, Jonah realized he had seen his own reflection in the window of the haberdashery store. Jonah smiled, amused at the start he'd given himself, and let vanity take over. He stopped abruptly and turned to admire his reflection.

A split-second later, he heard the chilling sound of a bullet zipping past his head, and the window shattered. Jonah acted on sheer instinct, throwing himself to the sidewalk. He snatched out a gun as he fell, landing on his belly. A woman screamed, and the horses tethered nearby snorted and stamped. A second bullet thudded into the wooden frame of the haberdashery store. The boards of the sidewalk shifted beneath Jonah as bystanders ran for cover. Jonah took no notice, intent on finding the person shooting at him. He peered between the legs of a wildly braying burro tied to the rail just where he was lying. As the burro moved, Jonah saw a man crouching on the opposite side of the street, half-hidden behind a pile of lumber.

Jonah lined his shot carefully, all too aware of the other people in the area. He fired, and saw a mass of splinters fly from the top board on the lumber pile. His assailant jerked away from the near-miss, showing more of himself. Jonah felt a jolt of surprise in recognizing the friend of German Spencer, the miner who had beaten Red Pearl about four months back. Jonah scowled at the figure across the wide street. He'd chased down men who had committed all kinds of crimes, and was still amazed by the capacity of some people to hold grudges. He didn't let his thoughts distract him from the important business of aiming for a second shot. It was long range for an accurate pistol shot, but Jonah could be grateful that the miner wasn't armed with a rifle.

His second bullet ripped the battered hat from Green's head. Green, the miner, ducked out of sight, so Jonah took the opportunity to roll sideways, bringing himself close to the end of the sidewalk. He was aligning his revolver again when Green's head popped up at a different part of the lumber pile. Green fired again, his bullet sending the burro into a bucking fit, and scraping the sidewalk just where Jonah had been lying before. Jonah took a snap shot and missed by a hand's breadth. It was enough to break the miner's nerve. Green vanished for a few moments, then sprinted out from the far end of the lumber pile.

The burro blocked Jonah's line of sight briefly as he scrambled to his feet. When he saw Green again, the miner had unfastened the reins of a chestnut horse, and was throwing himself into the saddle. Jonah leaped out into the street past the burro as Green got afork his mount and turned it to run. Jonah stopped moving and lifted his gun to shoulder-height to aim the long shot. His bullet grazed the rump of the chestnut, which squealed and threw itself into a twisting buck. Green didn't yet have both feet fully in the stirrups. He flew off and landed hard, face-down on the street. There was a slightly muffled gunshot and Green screamed. The chestnut fled, still bucking and kicking its heels.

Jonah sprinted towards the miner, who had rolled onto his side and was clutching at his crotch and thigh. As Jonah got close, he could see bright blood pumping from the wound torn in the man's leg. Green had pushed his pistol down the front of his trousers to free his hands for managing his horse. The fall had caused the gun to fire, sending a bullet through his lower belly and left thigh.

'For God's sake, help me,' Green moaned.

'You were sure doing your best to kill me not a minute back,' Jonah pointed out. He crouched down, keeping his gun from Green's reach while he pulled the revolver from the waistband of the miner's trousers, and carefully dropped it at arm's length. Green was dying fast, but Jonah wasn't about to take any chances.

'Better say any prayers you know,' he told Green, looking down at Green's white face. Green's moans were fainter, and his eyes were losing focus.

Footsteps caught Jonah's attention, He turned to see Marshal Tapton approaching, a shotgun held across his body.

'Ain't you gonna use them doctor skills you told me about?' the marshal challenged him.

Jonah shook his head. 'The bullet's torn open his femoral artery. Might just have well as cut his own throat. There's nothing I can do for him.' He glanced round at Green and saw that the miner had lost consciousness. Jonah stood and faced the marshal.

'So who in hell is he anyhow?' the marshal demanded.

'Now I don't rightly know his name,' Jonah admitted as he straightened his hat and brushed dust from his coat. 'He's a friend of German Spencer; took his side when I went to fetch Spencer in. I guess he figured to get even for his friend.'

The marshal's face got sourer than usual. 'That's your word on it?'

Jonah didn't bother getting riled over the slur on his honesty. 'There's plenty of folk at the Lucky Dog who saw Green and Spencer both try to clean my plough but good. And I'm sure you can find some witnesses none too far away from here who'll tell you that Green fired the first shot just now.'

Marshal Tapton grunted. 'Can't see no reason to go round bothering folk for statements.' He prodded Green with his shotgun. 'Especially over a fellow who's died of a bad case of stupidity.'

'I couldn't have put it better myself,'

Jonah agreed. He tipped his hat to the marshal. 'Now if you'll excuse me.' And he walked away briskly, leaving the marshal to deal with the bloodied corpse.

★   ★   ★

As Jonah had expected, it proved easier to find the record of Goff's mining claims, than to find the man himself. He set out early the next morning, riding upstream along the south fork of the Animas. It was another clear, brilliant spring morning, but his grey horse was picking its way through snow before long. The mountains reared their dazzling heads to either side as Jonah and his horse made slow but steady progress up the steep-sided gulch. There were few signs of human habitation here; just a scattered handful of prospectors' shanties clinging to the side of the mountain. The pounding of the mills was soon left behind, and Jonah was able to enjoy the chorus of bird song that filled the air.

Two hours of riding over increasingly steep terrain brought Jonah close to Slagle Basin, on the side of Emery Peak, where Goff had been prospecting. Jonah brought his blowing horse close to a wall of rock and jumped off, landing calf-deep in snow.

'Good feller, Cirrus,' he said, patting the horse's sweaty neck. 'You can rest here while I go scout on foot.'

Jonah didn't leave immediately, but loosened the girth and walked the horse in small circles until it had cooled down some. He unrolled a blanket fastened behind the saddle, and threw it over the horse's quarters. With his mount taken care of, and beginning to crop the thin grass, Jonah collected his rifle and set off on foot.

His progress was even slower now, for not only was the going steep, but Jonah wanted to avoid leaving an obvious trail behind him in the snow. He worked his way up into the basin, now and again using the stock of his Winchester as a staff. It was a relief when the ground flattened and Jonah found himself peering around rocks into the horse-shoe of Slagle Basin, with its steep sides rising to saw-tooth ridges. The blue sky above was reflected in the small, crescent lake that sat on the open floor of the basin. Jonah had never been along the south fork of the Animas before, but his careful study of the map in the land office had paid off. This was where Goff had registered his claim.

There wasn't much to be seen yet: a log hut, half-buried in snow, with a lean-to stable built on the side, a spoil heap of worthless rock and a small lumber building that covered the entrance to the mine workings. Not that there was much of a mine here yet. Jonah Durrell had never been interested in prospecting, he preferred his gold and silver to have 'In God We Trust' stamped on it, and a number to indicate its value. He was smart though, and during the last two years in Colorado, had picked up a fair understanding of hard-rock mining. There was no mechanization at this mine yet, no steam-driven hoist to lift the ore from the tunnel. Jonah could see layers of frozen snow in the heap of gangue by the mine entrance. The top of the rock pile was more recent than the last snowfall. No doubt Goff had wintered out here, digging his claim and collecting ore to be milled and processed when the snow had cleared enough to get it to town.

Jonah began working his way closer to the buildings, keeping himself out of sight as much as possible. Deep pathways had been cleared through the snow between the buildings. As Jonah got close to the mine, he could hear a rattling and squeaking that he guessed was the sound of the windlass in the mine building being used. Jonah took advantage of the noise to cover the sound he made on the snow, and got closer. A thundering rattle told him that ore was being transferred from the bucket on the windlass to something else. Jonah reached the cover of a couple of scrubby pines and some buffaloberry and crouched in their shadow to watch.

A man emerged from the door of the mine building and stood blinking in the sunlight for a few moments before trundling his crude wheelbarrow over to the spoil heap. He was medium height, with shoulder-length brown hair and a beard trimmed short on the cheeks but long in front. Jonah grinned to himself as he recognized the deep-set eyes, low, bushy eyebrows and prominent upper teeth he'd seen in the sketch of Goff on the wanted dodger. Goff was wearing a loose, mud-stained coat over his stained woollen trousers and frayed jacket, and sported a greyish hat with a sagging, uneven brim. Reaching the spoil heap, Goff began sorting the rock he'd brought up, singing to himself in a baritone voice that was pleasant when he hit the right notes.

He had his back to Jonah, his attention on the rock he was efficiently sorting. Jonah rose out from his cover, rifle aimed at Goff's back, and moved as fast as he could without making too much noise. He got to within ten feet before Goff started to look around.

'Don't try anything, you're under arrest,' Jonah said clearly.

Goff let a lump of ore fall back into the wheelbarrow and turned slowly.

'Who in hell're you?' he demanded, squinting towards Jonah, who had the sun at his back.

'I'm Jonah Durrell. There's a warrant out for your arrest over the killing of a gambler named Jacobi. I'm taking you back to Motherlode.'

'The tinhorn was a cheating skunk,' Goff stated irritably.

'I don't give a damn,' Jonah answered cheerfully. 'My job's to take you back and let a jury sort it out.'

'A goddam manhunter,' Goff said scornfully.

'And good enough to earn fancy clothes and this smart rifle,' Jonah replied. 'So turn around and lie on your belly, with your hands together behind you. Slowly.'

Goff did has he was told, cursing aloud all the while. Jonah took no notice, moving forward cautiously to stop just out of Goff's reach. There was much less snow here, most of it trampled down hard, but it would hamper any sudden movement from Goff as he lay prone. Jonah took his left hand off the rifle and reached into his overcoat pocket for a pair of hand-cuffs. A movement, glimpsed from the corner of his eye, grabbed his attention. A shadow was moving on the banked snow; the shadow of someone behind him. Jonah let go of the cuffs and started to turn, getting his left hand back on the Winchester.

Goff's partner moved in close, swinging his shovel at Jonah's head. Jonah instinctively threw up the rifle to block the shovel. The impact jarred dead leaves and animal muck from the shovel, splattering them onto his face and shoul-der. The unpleasantness distracted Jonah for a moment, letting Goff's partner pull back his shovel for another swing. Jonah blocked again, almost too late this time. He caught the impact close to his body and it pushed him off-balance. There was no time to turn the rifle and use it to shoot. There was no time either to pay attention to Goff. Jonah's full attention was on defending himself from the fast blows launched by the other miner. The miner knew his shovel well, and was an expert in swinging a hammer or a pick.

Jonah's Winchester was taking a battering, and his forearms were starting to ache from absorbing the blows. Catching the shaft of the shovel on his rifle again, he pressed back, trying his strength against the other man's. The miner was strong, but Jonah was taller. Jonah leaned into the wrestling match, gritting his teeth with the effort as he shoved. The miner began to give way, but as Jonah moved his weight forward, his foot slipped on the snow.

Jonah suddenly dropped, twisting to

his right as he lost his balance. From pushing down on the shovel, he managed to push it up and away as he fell. He landed on his back, snow getting into his hair and inside his coat collar. Jonah didn't notice. He brought the rifle up, bracing himself to catch the shovel as it swung down towards his face. The reflexes that made him so fast on the draw saved his life again. Jonah got his arms fully straight before the edge of the shovel crashed into the wooden grip of his rifle. The impact jarred him back into the snow, but the shovel stopped dead. Grunting with the effort, Jonah rolled to his right, twisting the rifle to try and tear the shovel from the other man's grip. The miner rapidly changed grip, swinging the shovel away and raising it. He took a short step forward and plunged it straight down, aiming for Jonah's head.

Jonah snatched the rifle back up again as he rolled the other way. The Winchester collided with the shovel as it drove downwards, deflecting it just enough that it caught the brim of his hat before hitting the ground just a couple of inches away. Jonah's heart was thudding fast with the exertion, and the fear from the near-miss, but he didn't have time to think about it. As the miner yanked the shovel out from the earth and snow, Jonah twisted himself around and kicked the man's leg. The miner yelled as he lost his balance. He skidded around in the hard-packed snow, taking one hand off the shovel as he tried to keep upright. Jonah rolled to his knees and got his rifle aimed at the miner just as the other man regained his balance.

'Throw that damned shovel over there before I put some daylight into you,' Jonah snapped.

They were still very close, close enough that the miner only had to take half a step to reach Jonah with his shovel. The battered rifle was aimed steadily at the miner's head. Both men knew that Jonah could fire a fatal shot before a blow from the shovel would reach him. The miner slowly lifted the shovel one-handed and tossed it where Jonah had indicated by a slight nod of his head.

'You got nothing on me. I ain't wanted for nothin',' the miner said, his pale blue eyes insolent.

'How about sheltering a fugitive and common assault?' Jonah replied, getting to his feet in a graceful motion. The aim of his rifle never changed. 'Open your coat. I want to be sure you've not got anything packed away under there.'

He also wanted to know where Goff had gone. Jonah had seen him heading for the log cabin, or its lean-to stable, while he had been fighting. It was possible that Goff had lit out while Jonah had been on the ground. Right now though, Jonah needed to concentrate on the man in front of him.

'Who are you?' he asked.

'M'name's Oldfield,' the miner grunted. Oldfield's face was dominated by flaunting red whiskers, which drew attention from his lumpy nose and narrow-set eyes. He grinned at Jonah, showing tobacco-stained teeth. 'I'll give you fifty shares in the mine, if you let me go,' he offered. 'Our ore assayed at five hundred dollars a ton. There's no reward for me, you won't get anything iffen you take me back to town.'

'I'll get the satisfaction of seeing you behind bars,' Jonah answered. 'Now open your coat.'

When he was satisfied that Oldfield was unarmed, Jonah handcuffed him and walked with him to the log cabin. The lean-to stable was empty; Goff had taken the mule and fled. His tracks were clear enough, and Jonah made a mental note of Goff's most likely route out of Slagle Basin, but there was no point in immediate pursuit. It would take the best part of an hour for Jonah to fetch his horse and bring it up to this point. More importantly, he didn't want to take off on a chase after a dangerous man while single-handedly watching over a prisoner. Jonah glanced at the brilliant blue sky, gauging the amount of daylight left, and started Oldfield on the walk back down. Jonah Durrell had no reason to hurry after Goff. He thought about getting back to Mother-lode and seeing Miss Jenny and her girls again. Jonah smiled to himself.

6

Jenny put her pen back in the holder next to the silver ink-stand, and picked up a pencil to make some calculations on the blotting paper. The only sounds in her little office were the soft rustling of her fawn-coloured dress and the ticking of a dainty carriage clock on the mantelpiece. Jenny bit softly on her lower lip as she wrote numbers in her flowing hand, adding the weekly staff wages for her parlour-house. Her thoughts were interrupted by a knock at the door. Jenny concentrated for a moment, muttering under her breath as she added numbers together, then she rapidly wrote her answer and looked up.

'What is it?'

The door opened halfway and one of the maids looked in. 'Mr Sharpe's here,' she said.

Jenny glanced at her paperwork, then decided a break would be a welcome idea. 'Show him in, Susie, and fetch us some coffee, please.'

As the maid closed the door and left, Jenny closed her ledgers and tidied her desk. Only then did she stand up to glance into a little wall mirror and to fluff up her hair.

'Good afternoon, Miss Jenny.' Adam Sharpe greeted her with a wide smile and took her outstretched hand. 'It's good to see you again.'

'Thank you.' Jenny gracefully withdrew her hand from his rather firm grip, and indicated that he should sit down. She moved her own chair to one side of the desk, closer to where Sharpe was sitting.

He removed his hat and set it on the desk, overlapping the ledgers.

'I came to see how you all were keeping after Miss Lucy's buryin' yesterday.' Sharpe said. 'I heard tell that Miss Linda done left town this morning.'

'That's right,' Jenny answered. 'She decided to head out west to California.'

'Did you think about going out there too?' Sharpe asked. 'I hear the weather's for sure better than up here,' he added with a smile.

Jenny shook her head. 'The big boom in California's over. There's fewer prospectors ready to throw their gold around, and more women for them to throw it at. There's plenty of good parlour-houses there already and they won't want a newcomer setting up shop. I could find myself being forced to take on 'partners' I didn't want.' Her defiance began to change to enthusiasm. 'This part of Colorado is just about to boom. The treaty with the Utes means there no real Indian trouble, like there is in Dakota territory. I can get in early and grow with the town, like you aim to.'

'You're a mighty shrewd woman, Miss Jenny,' Adam Sharpe said.

He spoke warmly enough, but Jenny couldn't see any warmth in his blue eyes. 'And a worker too, I guess. Did I interrupt you?' Sharpe asked, looking at the account ledgers on the desk.

'I see book-keeping as a necessary evil,' Jenny answered. 'I was ready for a break.'

'If you can do the ordering and book-keeping for a business like this, with what, twenty workers, you could easily find work in almost any company.'

Jenny looked at him steadily. 'Most companies prefer to hire men for book-keeping. Besides, this is my own business. I'd rather be looking after my own money than someone else's.'

Sharpe nodded. 'I can understand that of course, though it always seems strange to me to see a lovely lady running a business like a man.'

'Things are different out West,' Jenny emphasized. 'I encourage all my girls to learn things that'll help them when they get tired of this business.' She leaned forward in her chair as she spoke. 'I get them to teach one another. Some need help with reading, writing and figuring. Miss Sandy teaches piano and singing. They learn plain sewing, dressmaking, embroidery, baking and preserving, and good manners.'

'I guess some of them get snapped up as wives,' Sharpe said.

'Some do.'

'The lucky ones?'

Jenny half-smiled. 'I hope they've been lucky with their husbands. I often think that a good business and your own banking account is a more reliable source of happiness.'

Sharpe shook his head at such cynicism. 'In any case, Miss Jenny, what about your own business? When are you opening again?'

'Tomorrow evening,' Jenny answered, relaxing back into her chair.

There was a knock on the door before the little maid came in, carrying a tray with two cups of coffee, cream and sugar, all in a matching porcelain set. Sharpe made a sound of appreciation as he carefully took the dainty cup.

'These little feminine touches are what a man longs for,' he remarked. 'It's sure a pleasure to find such things out in a woolly mining town like this.'

'I know,' Jenny grinned. 'Men like to see curls and ribbons and lace but they don't always realize how much they like it unless it's paraded in front of them. Which is what I'm planning for tomorrow, to let Motherlode know I'm open for business again.' She paused to stir her coffee. 'I'm aiming to use Panhandle Street as my shop window, noon tomorrow. I'll be driving a carriageful of girls up and down Panhandle Street, all waving and blowing kisses and tempting men into my house of sin.'

Sharpe was silent for a moment, before suddenly smiling and exclaiming. 'That'll sure be one purty sight!'

'That's the plan,' Jenny said lightly. In spite of her tone, she had the distinct impression that Sharpe was holding something back from her. There seemed to be an undercurrent to his questions and his smile switched on and off as he needed to use it. Jenny was starting to feel uncomfortable with his interest in her business. She took a sip of her coffee and decided to turn the tables on him. There was no harm in learning what she could about the saloon trade. Smiling politely, Jenny asked Sharpe about his liquor suppliers.

* * *

Panhandle Street was a busy place at noon on a weekday, dominated by the men who filled the buildings and sidewalks. There were prospectors, buying kit, angling for a grubstake or trying to sell shares in their claims. Carpenters and labourers swarmed over the lumber buildings as the long street expanded and gaps between buildings were filled. A muleskinner led his string of laden animals towards the freight company depot. Unoccupied men sat in the sun, drinking beer, talking, and watching the bustle of the growing town. Only a handful of women were to be seen. A mother stood outside the post office with her daughter, reading aloud a precious letter from distant family. They wore neat, respectable clothes of muted fawn and blue.

The sober, hard-working atmosphere was shattered by the appearance of a carriage and team at the north end of Panhandle Street. A pair of matched, prancing chestnuts drew an elegant open-topped landau. This was no working vehicle, but a graceful, light carriage with a curving body painted dark green, with gold detail. Jenny sat on the box, whip in one hand and reins in the other as she guided the horses down the busy street. Miss Erica sat beside her, and four more of Jenny's girls were inside, waving to the startled, admiring men they passed.

They were a fine, enchanting sight: full skirts billowing in the confines of the carriage and ribbons fluttering from hair and parasols. Their dresses were modest in cut, but rustled with the sweet sound of silk and taffeta, and were as colourful as a cottage flower-garden. The girls laughed and called to the men who turned to watch them as the carriage made its slow progress along the rutted street.

Jonah Durrell was one of those who looked up to watch them pass. He was outside his hotel, checking his horse's hoofs and tack before setting out to find Goff. Oldfield, Goff's partner, was in the town jail, awaiting trial. Marshal Tapton hadn't been too keen on pressing charges of assault, but hadn't been able to deny that Oldfield had been sheltering a fugitive. Jonah temporarily pushed aside his plans for finding Goff in the pleasure of watching Miss Jenny and her girls. He turned around and leaned against his horse, studying the four girls inside the landau.

Three of them were fair-skinned blondes and the bright sun glinted off their uncovered heads. Miss Sandy, a lively New Englander, was leaning over the side and mischievously blowing kisses at a well-fed businessman who was walking alongside his wife. Beside her was Miss Megan, a slender elegant girl with hair of the palest yellow, which was so long and thick she could have ridden through the streets like Lady Godiva, sheltered only by the glory of her hair. Today Miss Megan was wearing a brilliant wine-red dress which set off the pale gold of her hair to perfection.

Sitting opposite them, facing the box, were Miss Helen and Miss Tania. Miss Helen was also fair, with an exquisite face and air of vulnerability that drew both men and women to her. It went alongside a startling innocence about her own attractiveness. She was waving to the men they passed, smiling with genuine pleasure and surprise at the admiration she drew. Most of the laughter and the shrieks of delight came from Miss Tania, a Brazilian beauty. Her silky café au lait skin and flashing dark eyes stood out in delightful contrast to the fair girls around her. The wild corkscrews of her dark hair had been subdued into an elaborate braided style, but a few shorter tendrils had escaped, and blew around her oval face as she chattered vigorously in accented English.

Jonah lifted one hand to wave at the vivid carriageful, thinking how they brightened the street. Most of the men present no doubt shared his opinion, but Jonah knew that some would disagree. His smile widened as Miss Sandy started singing a vulgar music-hall song. She was a fine singer, and took great delight in the teasingly suggestive lyrics. Jonah glanced along the street, amused by the reactions of those around. His attention was caught by a familiar shape, standing out front of the Shovel saloon next door. Jonah could only just see him around a delivery wagon waiting in front of the saloon. The bulky man was turned away from the street and was slightly hunched over. At first, Jonah thought the man was lighting a cigarette. He was pretty sure that it was Barker, the man who had attacked him in the Silver Lode a couple of days ago. As Jonah watched, the man turned and raised his arm. Jonah's first reaction was to look at the man's face and confirm his identity. In the moments it took him to do that, Barker had thrown something towards the carriageful of women. Jonah straightened in a hurry, hands automatically moving towards his guns. He saw something small land between the front wheels of the landau. Two seconds later, the firecracker exploded.

The cries of alarm from the women and bystanders were drowned by squeals of fear from the chestnuts drawing the carriage. The nearside horse started to rear, while the offside horse plunged forward into a panic-stricken gallop. The landau lurched to the left, throwing the women inside into a heap, and sliding Miss Erica and Jenny along the box. Then both horses were bolting along Panhandle street, dragging the landau behind them over the rutted, uneven ground. A frightened mule pulled itself loose from a hitching rail and began bucking in the street. Half-a-dozen mules and burros began braying, adding to the din and confusion.

Jonah spun around, unhitched his horse and vaulted into the saddle. Cirrus turned and jumped into a run even as Jonah was still getting his feet into his stirrups. All along Panhandle Street, drivers and riders were trying to clear the way. A delivery boy turned his little wagon and pony in beside the meat market, while a pair of heavy-legged horses struggled to get their laden wagon as close to the sidewalk as possible. Further ahead, Jonah could see a crowd of burros, each dragging lumber pit props for the mine, all milling in the centre of the street. Dismissing them for the moment, Jonah turned his attention to the racing carriage.

Jenny had her feet braced against the footboard and was hauling two-handed on the reins she had almost dropped when the landau lurched. Miss Erica was clinging to the seat back with one hand, and hanging on to Jenny's bustle with the other, as Jenny had no hand to spare. None of the women were screaming now, all aware that it would frighten the horses further. Instead, Miss Sandy had turned around and was kneeling on the leather seat, trying to reach over the folded hood towards the box. Swearing audibly, she hitched up her full skirts with one hand, while clinging to the hood with the other, and got her feet underneath her so she was standing on the seat. Miss Megan had also turned and took a handful of Miss Sandy's dress as Miss Sandy leaned further forward.

Jonah realized she was reaching for the brake lever. Jenny couldn't take her hands from the reins to reach it herself. As Miss Sandy leaned precariously over the front of the jolting carriage, Jonah urged his horse to catch up. Miss Tania slid herself into the footwell between the seats, and took hold of Miss Sandy's ankles. Miss Sandy strained forward, her hand inches from the brake lever. The landau's wheel hit a pothole, dropping the carriage suddenly, then bouncing back. Miss Sandy was thrown forwards, landing belly down across the folded hood, her draped skirts in disarray. Only the firm hold of the other women stopped her from toppling out. Miss Sandy swore and Miss Tania breathlessly recited a prayer.

'Stay inside!' Jonah yelled. His horse was galloping hard and only a few feet behind the carriage now.

Dirt flew up from the chestnuts' hoofs as the panicked horses bolted along the street. They took no notice of the tug and release of the reins as Jenny struggled to control them. A man wearing bib overalls sprinted across the street and tried to catch the bridle of the offside horse. He snagged the rein with his fingers, but lost his balance and stumbled towards the galloping horse.

It shied away as the man fell against its shoulder and tumbled to the ground. The carriage lurched again with the horse's movement, throwing Jenny off-balance and jolting Miss Sandy back into her seat. The man sprawled, winded, as the landau's wheels passed within inches.

He wasn't out of danger yet, for he was in the path of Jonah's galloping horse. Cirrus cleverly shortened his stride to take off in the right place. The grey horse leapt clear over the fallen man, with a whisk of his tail, and galloped on. Jonah stayed with him, barely moving in his saddle. He gave his horse a swift pat on the neck, but his attention was on the swaying carriage just ahead. It was getting ever closer to the milling string of burros, and the unyielding pit props each one had lashed to either side.

Cirrus was alongside the landau now. The women inside were holding onto one another as well as the sides and the hood. Jonah glimpsed Miss Sandy's face, and saw the hard, anxious look. She'd seen the burros ahead, and knew what the carriage was running towards, but she was holding onto her nerve as tightly as she clung to the side of the landau. Jonah couldn't spare the time to reassure the women. He lashed his reins loosely to the saddlehorn, using his legs to steer Cirrus closer to the front wheel of the landau. Leaning sideways in his saddle, Jonah reached for the brake lever with both hands. He grasped it and drew it back, trying not to apply it too fast. The rubber brake pad squealed against the metal wheel rim, causing Cirrus to shy away from the landau. At the same time, the landau hit another rut in the street, and jerked in the other direction. Still holding the brake lever, Jonah was nearly pulled from his saddle. For a moment, he was vividly aware of the iron-shod carriage wheel beside him, and the horror of falling beneath those wheels. In another moment, he let go of the lever, and grabbed a handful of

Cirrus's mane, hanging alongside his horse for a few strides until he managed to struggle upright again.

Cirrus had slowed, losing the rhythm of his stride. However, the drag of the brake had started to slow the chestnut team. Jonah urged his horse on again, getting ever closer to the off-side horse. At last he was close enough to lean from his saddle again and grasp the noseband of the chestnut's bridle. Jonah threw his weight back in the saddle, telling Cirrus to pull up. The grey slowed sharply. Jonah clung to the saddle with his legs and one hand, hauling back on the carriage horse's noseband with his left hand. The chestnut reluctantly began to prop and slow, trying to shake its head free. The landau began to slew around to the right. The burros were only yards away now.

A miner leapt from the sidewalk and grabbed for the bridle of the near-side horse. He hung on as the horses dragged him, adding his weight to the forces slowing the team. One of the burros in the mob lifted its head and brayed mournfully, drowning the frantic curses of the handler. The horse that Jonah was holding pricked its ears and began to slow of its own accord. Jenny's voice carried above the noise, calm and soothing as she played with the reins. The team horses dropped from a canter to a jog, and then halted, blowing and covered in sweat and foam.

Jonah dismounted and stood by the head of the off-side horse, patting its neck and talking calmly to it, as the miner was doing to the other chestnut. Panhandle Street seemed suddenly quiet, in spite of the mob of burros and the crowds gathering. Jenny had clambered down from the box and walked rapidly towards Jonah. She bristled with energy, longing to run, to ask questions loudly, but aware of the need not to upset the horses again.

'Thank you,' she said, her look and

her voice saying more than the simple words. A quick glance told her that Miss Erica was thanking the charmed and proud miner who had taken the bridle of the other horse. Jenny let out a long sigh and shivered.

'Are you all right?' Jonah asked, gently taking hold of her arm.

Jenny raised a smile for him. 'I'm just shook up a little,' she admitted. 'Nothing a shot of whiskey won't fix.' She turned slightly to caress the horse's muzzle. 'I wonder what it was set them off like that? It sounded like we ran over a detonator cap someone dropped in the street.'

'It wasn't a detonator cap,' Jonah said brusquely. He'd been too busy worrying about the runaway team and the women to think about what had caused the whole shebang. Now he remembered seeing Barker throw the firecracker.

Jenny turned to look at him hard. 'You know what happened?'

Jonah nodded. 'And when I catch up

with the man who did it, I'm going to knock him sky-west and crooked.' With that firm promise, he mounted his horse and rode back down Panhandle Street.

7

Jonah remembered that Barker had been outside the Shovel saloon when he had thrown the firecracker, so he rode back there to look for him. There was no sign of Barker outside, so Jonah dismounted, hitched his horse to a rail, and entered. The Shovel was a long, narrow building, lacking windows at the sides and so rather dim. Jonah paused just inside the doorway, letting his eyes adjust to the low lighting as he looked around. The saloon was as busy at lunchtime as it would be in the evening. To one side was the steady rattle of the roulette wheel, and the voice of the keno roller calling the numbers on his game. The bar was especially crowded, but Jonah picked out the man he was looking for.

In a few quick strides, he reached Barker and seized his shoulder, pulling the man roughly backwards. Barker's beer splashed another man as Barker staggered and started to turn. Jonah gave him no chance to speak, but threw a punch that mashed Barker's lips against his teeth. Shouts of protest and query arose from the crowd around them.

'I saw you throw the firecracker under Miss Jenny's carriage,' Jonah spat. Then he launched into the attack again.

Furious as he was, Jonah Durrell didn't fight blindly. While Barker was still gathering his wits, Jonah grabbed his right wrist and slammed Barker's hand against the edge of the bar. The rest of the beer showered out as Barker dropped his glass. Hauling with his right hand, and shoving with the left, Jonah propelled Barker away from the bar and into a more open area. The other bar patrons moved away, leaving space for the fight to develop. Word had already spread about the runaway carriage, and feeling rose against Barker as Jonah's accusation was spread.

Jonah threw hard punches, getting his weight behind them as he battered Barker about the head and chest. After the first couple of blows, Barker pulled himself together and tried to retaliate. Jonah largely kept out of his reach; he was lighter on his feet and had longer arms. This time he wasn't fighting defensively. He bounced forward to attack, then dodged away, deflecting Barker's punches. Soon the cut by Barker's eye from their last fight had opened again, mingling with sweat as it trickled down his face. Blood was oozing from his nose and mouth too. Both men had bloody knuckles.

Barker had had enough. As Jonah threw another hard punch, Barker grabbed his wrist and jerked, pulling Jonah off-balance. As Jonah staggered to one side, Barker bent and pulled a knife from his boot. He brought the knife up in a sweeping slash that tore across Jonah's overcoat as Jonah hastily twisted away. The overcoat was fastened, with Jonah's guns underneath. Barker grinned nastily as he lunged forward, the knife aimed at Jonah's chest.

Jonah caught his balance and spun the other way, to his left this time. He moved like a dancer, unlike Barker, whose momentum carried him past his opponent. As he lunged past, Jonah continued to turn and lashed out with a kick. He hit Barker high on the back of the left leg. Barker staggered forwards and caught the toe of his boot on an uneven floorboard. He fell heavily towards a table, temporarily vacated to leave room for the fight. Barker grabbed for the edge of the table and missed. He hit the edge of the table with his chin, snapping his head back violently. Glasses, cards and chips bounced on the table as Barker slid off and landed motionless on the floor.

Jonah was the first to reach him. He took the precaution of stepping on the knife that Barker still clutched, as he knelt down. Barker's eyes were open, but it only took a few moments for Jonah to establish that the fall against the edge of the table had snapped Barker's neck. He lowered Barker's head, and closed the dead man's eyes. Jonah looked up at the gathered crowd.

'Best send for Marshal Tapton,' he said calmly.

★　★　★

By the evening, Miss Jenny was able to tell Adam Sharpe that she had quite recovered her spirits. 'I'm afraid I can't entertain you for very long,' she added. 'We're very busy tonight.'

'It sure sounds that way,' Sharpe commented, smiling as he ran a hand over his neat hair.

Even with the office door closed, they could hear the piano, Miss Sandy singing a bawdy song, and the laughter of women and men.

'I've told Miss Sandy she should work in music halls,' Jenny went on.

'There's good money in that if you know how to please folks. She says she's happy enough working here. She said I have better beds than the hotels.'

Sharpe laughed along with Jenny. 'She was one of the girls with you this afternoon, wasn't she? I reckon you're all plumb brave. I don't guess you got any idea why Barker threw that firecracker?' Sharpe did an admirable job of sounding casual as he asked the question. He had been worried sick when he'd first heard that Barker had been seen to throw the firecracker under the carriage. Sharpe's reaction to the news of the fight and Barker's death had been sheer relief.

Miss Jenny shook her head. 'I guess he didn't like prostitutes. Or maybe those with more money than him.'

Sharpe took up on her explanation. 'I'll bet my bottom dollar you're right. I know business is good in this town, but it looks to me like there's some folks who plain don't want you here.'

'Well, Barker's not going to bother us

any more,' Jenny pointed out, smiling cheerfully at Sharpe.

She seemed brighter and more energetic than Sharpe had seen her before. This evening, Miss Jenny was wearing a low-cut gown of glimmering amethyst silk, set off with gold embroidery and tiny crystals that twinkled in the lamplight as she moved. She was speaking briskly, smiling, and her dark eyes sparkled. She certainly didn't look as worried as Sharpe had planned.

'I don't reckon it was Barker that killed Miss Lucy though,' Sharpe said. 'Barker didn't match up to the description of the feller you gave the marshal.'

Jenny looked more thoughtful. 'That's so,' she admitted.

'Marshal Tapton and Jonah Durrell are no closer to finding the feller as killed Miss Lucy,' Sharpe went on, leaning forward as he spoke. 'Why, Durrell was off chasing after some prospector to earn himself the reward.'

'Well, yes. But then he's a man-hunter. It's what he does.'

Sharpe thought he heard doubt in Miss Jenny's tone. 'Of course that's what he does. It's sure lucky for you he was in town today, but you can't expect him to always be around. He'll go wherever there's an easy target for him to hunt. There's nothing to tie him to Motherlode. He doesn't own property here, like we do.'

Jenny shrugged philosophically. 'I'm used to looking after myself.'

'Well, if you need a shoulder to lean on, or someone to help you out if things get sticky, you know you can call on me,' Sharpe said with a roguish smile. 'And don't forget, if things get so bad you want to sell out, I want first refusal.'

Jenny laughed. 'I swear I'll remember, but I'm aiming to be here a long time, God willing and the creek don't rise.'

Sharpe made himself laugh in return. 'You sure got sand to burn, Miss Jenny.'

She smiled and leaned towards him, but was interrupted by a knock on the office door. At her answer, one of the parlour-maids entered.

'Jonah Durrell's here to see you, Miss Jenny.'

A brilliant smile spread across Jenny's face as she turned and rose. Sharpe wanted to scowl, but fought not to show his feelings. As Jenny greeted Durrell with a hug, Sharpe fiddled with the silver ring on the little finger of his right hand.

'You look a regular jewel tonight, Miss Jenny,' Jonah said, his liquid, dark eyes unashamedly flirting with her.

'I wouldn't be looking so bright if you hadn't acted so fast out on Panhandle Street,' Jenny answered. 'Me and my girls are truly grateful to you.'

'I got some ideas on how you can repay me,' Jonah said, peering down at her cleavage.

Jenny laughed. 'Dinner, and any of the girls you want, on the house.'

'Who says it's a girl I want?' Jonah

took hold of her waist.

Jenny firmly disentangled herself. 'I only have a single bed. It's the girls who are here to share theirs. You keep your ideas to yourself.'

In spite of her words, there was a flirtation in her tone that Sharpe had never heard directed at himself. He chose to interrupt things by standing up and drawing their attention his way.

'I'm right pleased to meet you again, Durrell,' he said, reaching to shake the other man's hand and turning on his charm. 'I reckon this whole town owes a debt to your quick thinking today. Motherlode's a sight better off without scum like Barker around.'

'I'd have settled for whaling the leather out of him,' Durrell answered. 'But I don't reckon he's going to be much mourned round here.'

'What did Marshal Tapton have to say?' Jenny asked.

Jonah shrugged. 'About as much as usual. There were plenty of witnesses to say that Barker drew his knife on me, and that he stumbled and fell against the table. The marshal wrapped it up as accidental death. It saves him the bother of a prosecution.'

Jenny snorted in an unlady-like manner. 'I swear I don't know how Tapton got the job of marshal. All he's good for is taking taxes, shooting stray dogs and making folks clear up piles of rubbish around their premises.'

'This can sure be a tough town to live in when things get rough,' Sharpe added slyly. Picking up his black hat, he bowed in Jenny's direction. 'Like you said, Miss Jenny, you're plumb busy tonight, and I'd best be seeing to my own place. So I'll say goodnight.' He managed a smile for Durrell too, and quit the parlour-house in a friendly way, but without lingering.

Outside, Panhandle Street was as lively as ever. As he paused to light a thin cigar, Sharpe could hear music and the buzz of noise from the saloons dotted up and down the long street. Sharpe inhaled deeply on the cigar, trying to clear his thoughts. There was plenty of business already in Motherlode, from the pool hall to the cribs where the cheapest whores lived and worked. Sharpe didn't like their sort; most of them addicted to drink or morphine. He wanted a share of a parlour-house like Jenny's, and wanted it so bad he'd ordered murder to try to scare her out.

Sharpe began walking, his boots thudding solidly on the uneven sidewalk as he strode along. His plans for scaring Miss Jenny out weren't working and she didn't want to sell. He would be willing to take her as a lover, if that would get him a share in her place, but she never looked at him in the way she did Jonah Durrell. Sharpe chewed on the end of his cigar as he thought of Durrell. He didn't want to admit to himself that he was jealous of Durrell. Instead, Sharpe thought about how Durrell was supporting Miss Jenny, and thwarting his plans for getting rid of her. Durrell's interference had already cost him Barker. The answer was simple enough. Sharpe had to get rid of Jonah Durrell: permanently.

★ ★ ★

The next morning though, Jonah was in fine spirits as he rode out of Motherlode and headed along the trail to Slagle Basin again. Last night there had been no interruptions to his time in Miss Erica's bedroom, and he felt confident that she had enjoyed herself as much as he had. As he rode through the fresh, clear air, Jonah's thoughts were mostly on the delightful dilemma of which of Jenny's young ladies he should choose next.

All such speculation was put aside when Jonah reached the point below the basin where he had left his horse before. He followed the same routine again, following the path he'd broken through the snow before until he was in sight of Goff's mine. Jonah stopped within cover of the trees, which masked the white clouds of breath he was producing, and took a good look around. There was plenty of birdsong, which was reassuring until the carolling of the chickadees was interrupted by the alarm cries of the jays.

Jonah stayed as still as he could, scanning the basin intently until a stealthy movement not far from the prospector's cabin caught his eye. He waited, and was rewarded with the sight of a fine lynx prowling cautiously around the cabin. Its huge, furry paws carried it easily over the snow as it inspected the cabin. Jonah had a brief thought to the value of its fur, but found more pleasure in watching the splendid cat warily inspect the mine. Its presence also reassured him that there were no other humans around.

After ten minutes of watching the big cat, Jonah was starting to feel cold, and was ready to go on with his work. He stood up, not taking any particular trouble to move quietly. The lynx's tufted ears swivelled in his direction, followed by a glance from the green-gold eyes. As Jonah stepped out of the trees, the lynx was off, running in bounds across the snow, back the way it had come. Confident that there was no one hidden in ambush, Jonah examined the tracks around the mine and cabin.

The snow blanket was beginning to melt during the day, but froze again at night. Jonah Durrell now had plenty of experience at tracking in snow, and soon had a good idea of what had happened here since his last visit. The marks of his fight with Oldfield were already losing their shape and were overlaid with the tracks of animals. Goff had returned yesterday, with a mule and a burro. He'd scouted around some, on foot, then had loaded up the mule and burro and returned the way he'd come. If Jonah hadn't gotten delayed by the runaway landau, he most likely would have been here to intercept Goff.

Jonah investigated the log cabin, wrinkling his nose in distaste at the smell of unwashed bodies and clothes that lingered after the winter occupation. A quick search showed him that basic utensils like the coffee pot and frying pan had been taken, along with some of the food stores like sugar and coffee. The sacks of meal and flour stood open, with some of the content scattered carelessly around. The spilled stuff was fresh though, suggesting that Goff had hurriedly transferred some of the foodstuffs to smaller bags during his brief return. Open sacks and spilled food would attract vermin. It looked to Jonah as though the two miners normally kept their food supplies tidy. So if Goff hadn't laden his animals with full sacks of food, what had they been carrying?

Jonah pushed aside the grubby blanket that served as a door, and stepped into the lean-to stable. Dried grass bedding had been swept to one end, and muck was partially gathered together, just as Oldfield had left it when he went to attack Jonah. Full sacks, carefully stacked, took up the far end of the stable. Jonah smiled, and went to investigate. The sacks were full of ore, the product of a long winter's work. Sacks of ore were what Goff had loaded his animals with, and he must have been furious at having to leave the rest behind. Jonah left the sacks, and went back through the cabin, pausing to fasten the sacks of food left behind. Then he went outside, leaving behind the dim and smelly cabin to take a welcome breath of the invigorating mountain air.

With the deep snow, it didn't take much effort to find where Goff had entered and left the basin. His tracks led north-west over the ridge that separated Slagle Basin from McCarty Basin to the north. From there, Goff would have ridden north-west along the valley that ran parallel to the one that Jonah had taken to reach this basin. Both valleys opened into Eureka Gulch. Jonah studied the ridge and the mountains beyond. Goff's route to

Eureka Gulch was probably shorter, but using it would mean fetching Cirrus up from where he'd left the horse below Slagle Basin, and riding over the steep, snowy ridge. Jonah knew he would make better time riding back along the south fork of the Animas. His horse would make better time there than it would climbing over a difficult trail more suited to Goff's burro and mule. With his next move clear in his mind, Jonah waded through the snow, back to his horse.

8

An hour or so of steady riding brought Jonah to the mouth of the valley below McCarty Basin. It didn't take long to find the tracks of Goff's animals, leaving the valley and heading up Eureka Gulch, away from Motherlode. Jonah tried to guess where Goff would be heading. The prospector would be thinking of somewhere to sleep in shelter, and somewhere to sell his ore and buy more supplies. He might even try selling his claim before leaving the area. The main choices were Silverton and Animas Forks. Jonah guessed Animas Forks, to the north. When Goff's tracks left the gulch to follow a track leading northwards over a ridge, Jonah laughed aloud. He celebrated by pulling a strip of dried beef from a paper bag in his coat pocket, to chew on as he rode.

Animas Forks was a lively town perched on the shoulder of Treasure Mountain. As he rode in, Jonah could see a train of burros heading out along the trail to Ouray, and another coming in over Cinnamon Pass to the east. Two mills that serviced the local mines dominated the town with their size and their noise. The town itself boasted a post office, saloon, general store, a hotel, and about thirty lumber cabins. Jonah didn't go straight into Animas Forks, but first rode to the nearest mill. There, he made his way to the manager's office, leaving his horse hitched to a post outside.

The office seemed stuffy after the fresh mountain air, and there was a faint, acrid haze which suggested that the pot-bellied stove in the corner wasn't drawing properly. Jonah introduced himself to the mill manager, who looked pleased to be diverted from his paperwork, and promptly offered coffee before Jonah could even state his business.

Seated in a plain wooden chair, and with the cup of coffee warming his hands, Jonah described Goff to Delaine, the manager, and explained why he was looking for him. Delaine nodded vigorously and had to push his gold-rimmed glasses back up his nose.

'He stopped by here yesterday afternoon, sure enough,' Delaine said. 'Had him a couple of sacks of ore he was wanting to sell. Had him an assay certificate but I told him I wasn't taking no one else's certificate.' Delaine leaned across his desk towards Jonah and dropped his voice. 'Some folks forge certificates, you know, or steal them.' He shook his head sadly and sat back.

Jonah was enjoying the coffee and was in no hurry to move. 'What did you do?'

'I told him we'd have to assay a sample here before I could fix on whether to buy or not. The company don't usually buy small quantities from prospectors, but Goff said he needed a grubstake real bad.' Delaine nodded again. 'Offered to sell out the mine, too but I told him I couldn't think on it till we got the assay results. I thought right from the get go there was something not right with that feller and now I know for sure.' He smiled, looking pleased with himself.

'Did you tell him when you'd get the results of the assay?' Jonah asked.

Delaine nodded hard again, and caught his spectacles as they slid off his nose. 'I told him to come back late this afternoon, or tomorrow morning.' He held on to the spectacles absent-mindedly and blinked across the desk at Jonah as he spoke. 'Do you want to stay here and wait for him?'

Jonah sipped coffee and considered the question. Goff was surely in Animas Forks, just a five-minute ride away. He might not show up at the mill for another four hours, at best. It shouldn't take too long to find Goff in a town the size of Animas Forks, and with any luck, they could be back in Motherlode before nightfall.

'I'll head into town,' Jonah decided. Finishing the coffee, he put the cup on the desk and stood up. 'You've been real helpful,' he said, with a warm smile.

'Not at all, not at all,' Delaine insisted. 'One way or another, we got to have law to protect our interests. I shall be most interested to see if the ore Goff wants to sell assays the same as on the certificate he showed me. He claimed it was worth ninety dollars per ton.'

Jonah toyed with the idea of bringing the remaining sacks of ore from Slagle Basin and selling them to the mine himself. However, Goff's partner would most likely be out on bail soon, and none too pleased at finding his winter's work missing. On reflection, Jonah decided that the value of the raw ore wasn't enough to outweigh the hazard of having Oldfield after his hide. With a small sigh, he dismissed the idea of picking up some extra money. He set his hat back in place and made his farewell.

Jonah reached Animas Forks very soon. The earlier hours of riding and searching paid off in the first saloon that he visited. He paused just inside the door of the crude, lumber building, to let his eyes adjust to the dim light. The place was half-full, with the gambling tables doing the best business. As Jonah looked about, he saw Goff at a table with another man, talking urgently and proffering papers that looked like land registry certificates. Jonah swiftly unfastened his long coat and automatically checked the Smith & Wessons sitting in their holsters.

The man nearest to him saw the matched guns and backed away a little, setting off ripples of movement among the other drinkers, as Jonah began walking towards Goff. It may have been those movements that made Goff glance up from his conversation. He saw the tall man walking towards him and recognized Durrell immediately. Goff's chair fell backwards as he shot to his feet and raced to the back of the saloon. The man he'd been talking to looked around wildly as Goff fled and Jonah sprinted after him.

'Stop!' Jonah yelled, drawing his right-hand gun. There were too many people around for him to risk taking a shot on the run though, and Goff was most likely unarmed.

Goff reached the rear door of the building and shoved his way through. Jonah pounded after him, shouldering the door open and bursting through fast, in case Goff was waiting on the other side. He wasn't: Goff was running. Jonah caught a glimpse of him as he ran between two of the crude cabins that stood back of the buildings on Main Street. Jonah sprinted after him, his heavy overcoat flapping as he ran. As he reached the alley between the cabins, he saw Goff disappearing around the corner of the right-hand cabin. Resisting the urge to waste breath on cursing, Jonah followed.

He rounded the corner of the

building and saw Goff again, still clutching his certificates as he ran.

'Stop, or I'll shoot!' Jonah kept running as he shouted the warning.

Goff kept going, so Jonah took a shot on the run. He intended it mostly as a warning shot but it came within a foot or so of Goff's head, hitting the wall of a cabin. Goff flinched but ran on, ducking between cabins back in the direction of Main Street.

Jonah had already gained ground on Goff, but now he ran even faster. There were more people around on Main Street, and more opportunities for Goff to vanish. As he rounded the corner of the building too, Jonah found himself with a clear view of the fleeing miner. His view of Main Street beyond was partially obscured by some laundry; blankets hung out to dry on a line between the two cabins. In fact it was a double line, which fed through a pulley system attached to the cabin's walls, so the washing could be pegged out from an attic window. Goff had to run beneath the heavy, damp blankets to reach Main Street.

Jonah skidded to a halt, bringing his gun up to shoulder height. He sighted on the pulley fixed to the wall, and fired. The shot slammed into the cabin wall right where the pulley was attached, tearing up the wood. The pulley's fixings loosened, and the weight of the wet, woollen blankets tore it from the wall. The line collapsed and a grey and red striped blanket fell on Goff. It caught him off-balance as he ran, and knocked him to his knees as it folded around him. Jonah caught up as Goff struggled to free himself from the heavy folds of wool.

He pushed over the thrashing heap of blanket and dropped to his knees on top of his prisoner. Even through the thick blanket, Jonah could hear the gasp as Goff's breath was driven out of his chest. Jonah holstered his gun and fished his handcuffs from his coat pocket. Onlookers gathered at the end of the alley and watched as Jonah untangled a winded Goff from the blanket and cuffed him. When he had his prisoner under control, Jonah bravely summoned the full force of his charm for the more challenging task of pacifying the woman whose clean laundry had just been dropped into the street.

★   ★   ★

By late that afternoon, Jonah had successfully delivered his prisoner to Marshal Tapton back in Motherlode. Jonah wasn't altogether sure who had been the most unhappy about the situation: Goff, as he was locked into his small cell, or the marshal, who had to pay Jonah the reward and then start on the paperwork relating to Goff's capture, and his trial. The more gloomy the marshal looked, the more Jonah's spirits rose, and he left the office whistling cheerfully. After seeing his horse settled at the livery barn, and making some enquiries there, he returned to his hotel for a meal and a very welcome hot bath.

* * *

Miss Jenny thought that Jonah Durrell looked as spruce as a model in a catalogue advertisement when she greeted him later that evening. There were half a dozen other men in her parlour-house, all well-dressed, but none wore their clothes with the same flair that Jonah did. He was handsome, stylish and somehow very masculine in a way that made Jenny more aware of herself as a woman. She changed her mind about leading him into the music parlour, and instead escorted him into the privacy of her office.

'Have things been all right here today?' Jonah asked, sitting down.

Jenny nodded. 'No trouble of any kind. Some wines I'd ordered arrived today, and not a bottle broken.'

'Do you lose much stock on these trails?'

'It happens sometimes. It's a damn expensive business, setting up shop way out here.'

'And you're gambling that there's going to be enough trade to make it worthwhile,' Jonah said understandingly. 'You've invested as much in the success of the local mines as the mine owners have.'

They talked about Jenny's business for a few minutes, undisturbed by the muffled sound of music and voices from the parlour rooms. Jenny found Jonah a pleasure to talk business with. He wasn't trying to sell her anything, nor was he asking for favours or trying to extract a bribe. She felt strongly that he was interested in how she was doing, but as a friend, not as a rival. At length, she turned the conversation to his activities.

'Did you find the man you were after?' she asked, tucking a stray lock of dark hair behind her ear.

Jonah smiled and nodded. 'Brought him in alive and kicking, or at least grumbling. And the reward money is burning a hole in my pocket.'

Jenny gave him a mischievous look. 'Miss Erica again, or would you like to visit with another girl?'

Jonah smiled back. 'All of your girls are very tempting, but what I'd most like to do is to take you out for a buggy ride tomorrow, Miss Jenny.'

Jenny's eyes went round with surprise. For a moment, she wondered what he meant, but a longer look at his face told that he meant exactly what he'd just said.

'Are there any buggies in Motherlode?' She said the first thing that came into her head.

'The Colorado Livery's got a plumb fine one. I spoke to them about it this afternoon when I was stabling Cirrus.'

Jenny's face broke into a tremendous smile. 'I'd love to go out for a buggy ride. Thank you, Jonah.' Excitement bubbled up inside her, making her dark eyes sparkle.

Jenny had been born and raised in a

brothel. She'd helped with the chores from the time she was old enough to dust furniture, and on her fourteenth birthday, her virginity had been sold to the highest bidder. Her relationships with men had been centred around money, as maid, prostitute, madam and the owner of a business. Very, very rarely, had she ever simply been Jenny, a woman to be appreciated for her own sake.

'Don't thank me,' Jonah answered, smiling gently. 'It's my privilege.'

Jenny didn't know how to answer him, so she smiled, which was answer enough.

* * *

Later that same evening, Adam Sharpe had a visit from one of the ostlers who worked in the Colorado stables. The saloon owner was sitting at his private table, watching the evening's business, when he saw the ferrety ostler approaching.

Sharpe frowned. 'I already know

136

that's Durrell's back in town,' he said as the ostler stopped by the table. 'I knew that hours ago.'

The ostler rubbed his calloused hands together. 'Do you know what he'll be doing tomorrow?' His beady eyes gleamed with greed.

Sharpe took out his billfold and laid it on the table. It was a fat, expensive one, with his initials embossed on the black calfskin. The ostler smiled at the sight of it, revealing a row of crooked, yellow teeth.

'Durrell done booked the buggy and a hoss for tomorrow morning. Eleven o'clock,' the ostler added, holding out his hand.

'Did he say where he was driving?' Sharpe asked.

The ostler shook his head. 'He done said he'd be back by four at the outside.' Sharpe handed the man five dollars and dismissed him. Anger simmered up inside Sharpe as he sat still.

Durrell's successful return with the

miner had been irritating but bearable. This was worse: Sharpe could only think of one reason why Durrell would be hiring a buggy. No doubt Durrell was over at the parlour-house right now, working his charm on Miss Jenny. Sharpe wanted Jenny to turn to him, to come under his control so he could get his hands on that fancy cat-house. He thought about getting Jenny into his bed and doing what he wanted with her body. Sharpe wanted that control, which would be all the sweeter for her first resistance. But handsome, smooth-talking Jonah Durrell was getting in the way of those dreams. Sharpe needed to get rid of Durrell and then he could move in on Jenny. And she would pay for making him feel second-best.

Sharpe sat and thought for a minute, ignoring the girls dancing on the stage as he looked about. Spotting a balding man with a scarred lip, he beckoned him to the table to speak quietly.

'Find Marsh and Nickerson, and come to my office in ten minutes. No more drink for any of you tonight; you're going to need clear heads in the morning.' He spoke fiercely, cutting off any protest. 'The pay will be good if the job's done properly.'

A quick nod dismissed Hamilton, leaving Sharpe to begin fleshing out the details of his plan.

9

Miss Jenny was ready for Jonah the next day, prompt at eleven. He helped her into the lazy-back buggy, complimenting her on her stylish fawn dress and jacket, then loaded the basket of food that she had provided.

'I thought we'd drive north a spell,' he suggested, flicking the reins to start the hired horse moving. 'I saw some real pretty places along the valley when I was coming back from Animas Forks yesterday.'

'That sounds just fine to me,' Jenny answered happily. 'I've been up and down the trail to Silverton a half a dozen times, but I've never been north of town before.'

They left Motherlode behind inside of a minute, and followed the trail as it wound close to the river Animas. As the stands of dusky pine and new-greening cottonwoods surrounded them, Jenny sighed contentedly.

'You get so used to the mills pounding you stop hearing them after a while, but when you get out here, where you can't hear them, you remember what quiet really is.'

Jonah smiled but said nothing, content also to listen to the gentle sounds around them. As they were in no hurry to go anywhere in particular, he slowed the horse to a walk. The horse's hoofs thudded on the ground in a steady rhythm, matched by the quiet creaking of the leather harness and the noises of the buggy. They could hear the river too, rushing louder where it ran white over rocks and quieter in the deep pools made by beaver. There was plenty of birdsong to enjoy, and a pair of squabbling male catbirds flew across the trail, so close that the buggy horse laid its ears back and snorted.

After ten minutes of peace, they began to talk, quietly. Jonah talked about his childhood in Vermont, telling

Jenny about the country there, and his adventures with his brothers. Jenny laughed and asked questions, but Jonah noticed that she volunteered very little about her own childhood. Her reticence naturally piqued his curiosity, but he refrained from asking questions. An hour or so passed pleasantly until they reached the pretty meadow where Burns creek tumbled down from Niagara Peak to join the Animas.

Jenny was happy to stop when Jonah suggested having lunch. She spread a rug and got out the picnic while he unharnessed the horse, watered it at the creek, and hobbled it. The small meadow was bounded by dense trees and the river, so the horse was unlikely to wander far anyway, but Jonah didn't want to take a chance with a hired horse that he didn't know. The food was good, prepared by Ken, the parlour-house cook. Jonah ate well, drinking sparingly from the half-bottle of white wine that had been carefully packed.

'I declare, this is a real civilized way

to waste time,' he remarked, watching a bold chipmunk darting around in search of crumbs.

Jenny replied. 'I was once given a sampler that read 'Lost, between sunrise and sunset, one golden hour, set with sixty diamond minutes. No reward is offered, for it is gone forever'.'

Jonah snorted. 'That was said by someone with no imagination, and no sense of beauty. If we're lucky enough to live in a place as beautiful as this, it would be a sin not to take time to enjoy it.'

Jenny chuckled. 'I always hated that sampler. I took it with me when I left . . . home, and first chance I got, I burned it.'

Jonah laughed aloud. 'Miss Jenny, you are a woman of rare spirit.'

She flushed a little, evidently pleased by his compliment but unsure how to respond. Getting to her feet, she excused herself with the need to go into the bushes. Jonah watched her disappear among the scrub growth under the trees, and wondered whether to start packing up the remains of the picnic. He abandoned the idea, and lay back on the rug to enjoy watching the fluffy white clouds drifting by overhead.

The peace didn't last long. An angry exclamation from Jenny, and a sudden crashing in the bushes, brought Jonah to full alertness. He rolled over and started to rise, head turning in the direction of the noise. As Jonah got to his feet, Jenny appeared from around a scrubby willow, pushed by a man who held her arm twisted up behind her back. He was also holding a revolver to her side. Two more men emerged from the trees, a few feet to either side of Jenny and her captor, their handguns aimed at Jonah. Jonah stopped moving, his hands close to his guns, and stared bitterly at the man who held Jenny.

All three men wore bandannas pulled up to hide their faces. Their clothes were unremarkable; mostly brown, black and grey in colour. Jonah looked carefully at each one in turn, assessing the level of threat they posed.

'Unfasten that gunbelt nice and slow.' The man holding Jenny gave the order. 'Use your left hand, and toss it to your left.'

Jonah took a slow, deep breath, forcing himself to stay calm. The frustration of being bushwhacked added fuel to his fury at seeing a women being threatened. He wanted to protect Jenny, not surrender his guns and stand unarmed before these bandits.

Slowly, Jonah reached down to the buckle of his gunbelt.

As he obeyed the order, Jonah saw Jenny's free hand moving slowly too. She was reaching across herself with her left hand, reaching for the gun held against her side. Jenny was about five inches taller than the man holding her. That height would make it harder for the bandit to keep a secure grip on the arm he held twisted behind her. She needed to grab or deflect that gun held to her side, and she needed to do it unnoticed.

'I got plenty of money on me,' Jonah said loudly. He started to raise his left hand again, bringing his right hand slowly towards his chest. 'I won't put up a fight. You can take the whole billfold and leave without any trouble.'

He had their attention. The men were watching him as he reached for the inner pocket of his jacket. Guns raised slightly, taking better aim on him. He kept on talking, loud and fast.

'Don't get all jumpy now. There's nothing but a billfold in this pocket.' Jonah had to fight his compulsion to watch Jenny's stealthy movement. He turned his head slightly to look at the bandit on his left, drawing the other men's attention that way. Then Jenny's hand closed on her captor's gun and all hell broke loose.

Jonah dived forward, snatching out his left gun in mid-air, and hit the ground rolling. Shots erupted from around the clearing. Jonah came up onto one knee and fired at the man on his left. He saw the bandit jerk backwards, and lunged to his feet while drawing his other gun. A shot from the right zipped past him. Jonah ran forwards, looking right but firing both guns. He could see Jenny struggling with the third bandit, but had no time to help. More shots; the smell of black powder in the air. Jonah fired again at the man on his right and saw him reel and fall backwards, dropping his gun.

Before the bandit had hit the ground, Jonah spun the other way and dropped to one knee. A bullet cracked the air over his head as he sighted his left hand gun on the other bandit. One shot took the man down, and Jonah was on his feet again. Now he had time to help Miss Jenny, and help she needed.

The bandit had wrestled himself free and pushed her back into a shrubby willow, which had snagged her hair and clothes. Jenny was trying to pull herself free as the bandit raised his gun towards her, spitting curses. Jonah didn't waste breath on warnings or demands. He fired both guns together, blasting the bandit from his feet. The man landed untidily, his chest torn open and his blood starting to soak into the leaf mould beneath him.

Jonah sprinted across to Jenny, sparing a moment for a look at the dying bandit. Satisfied that there was no danger from him, Jonah gave his attention to the woman.

'Are you hurt?' He scanned her anxiously, looking for blood or other signs of injury.

'No.' Jenny started to shake her head and stopped as a twig pulled her hair.

'I'll come and help you in a minute,' Jonah said. 'I want to check on those other varmints first.'

He reloaded his revolvers, leaving the left one holstered, and went to examine the other two bandits. One had taken a bullet through the neck. He lay with his eyes open, dead within seconds. Jonah pulled the bloodied bandanna down and stared thoughtfully at the bandit. Leaving the corpse, Jonah crossed to the third man. He had taken a bullet across his shoulder, and another to the chest. The blood-soaked bandanna he wore over his face still stirred with his breathing as Jonah approached cautiously, but his breaths were shallow and growing weaker. Jonah used his foot to nudge the bandit's gun away from a limp hand, then crouched next to the man.

He tugged down the bandanna and studied the dying man's face. The bandit didn't react in any way. It hardly took Jonah's doctor skills to know that there was nothing that could be done for him. Jonah left the bandit to finish bleeding to death, and returned to Jenny. She had disentangled herself from the shrubby undergrowth and was crouching beside the leader of the bandits.

'I'm sorry I let him grab me and use me as a hostage like that,' she apologized, and looked at Jonah as he joined her.

'I reckoned we were safe enough here,' he answered, mastering his feeling of guilt to look her right in the face. 'I'm real sorry this happened.'

'It's no more dangerous out here than on the streets of Motherlode at night, or any other mining town,' Jenny said practically. She softened the mood briefly with a smile, before asking if he'd recognized the other two bandits.

'Not to put a name to,' Jonah replied. 'If we can find their mounts, we'll haul them back into town for the marshal.' Jonah grinned. 'I'm sure Marshal Tapton will love all the paperwork.'

Jenny grinned too. 'Let's take a look at this polecat,' she said, pulling the bandanna off the face of the corpse in front of her.

The face meant nothing to Jonah, but Jenny gasped softly, and studied the bandit's face, frowning.

'That's . . . I'm sure that's the man who killed Lucy. That man was clean-shaven, I remember . . . '

Jonah studied the moustache and side whiskers of the dead man. 'Some men could grow that length of whiskers in about a week.'

Jenny let out a long sigh. 'I'm sure that's him, Tom Halesworth, or who-ever he really was.' She looked at Jonah with tears sparkling in her bright, brown eyes. 'Thank you, Jonah. Lucy can rest easy now. That son-of-a-bitch won't hurt any woman ever again.'

*   *   *

Adam Sharpe couldn't settle to the business of calculating the week's wages. He stared at the column of figures blankly for almost a minute, and shook his head. Dropping the pencil on to the desk, he shoved his chair back and stood up. He roamed around the confines of his office, ending up by the window, where he stared out across an empty lot towards the laundry and the river. There, Sharpe took out his pocket-watch and checked the time, stifling a sigh.

Marsh and the other two should be

back any time soon. At odds of three to one, they could hardly fail to deal with Jonah Durrell, but could they follow orders properly? Sharpe began pacing again as he reviewed his meeting with them late last night. Sharpe's orders had been to make the killing look like a robbery. 'Kill Durrell and throw a scare into the woman.' He warned them, Marsh especially, that they weren't to hurt Miss Jenny, and not to give her a chance of recognizing them.

Sharpe seated himself at his desk again, then pulled out his pocket-watch once more. The slender hands had barely moved since the last time he'd looked at it. Sharpe snapped the watch-case down and shoved it back into his vest pocket. He took up the pencil and looked blankly at the sums once more, doodling spiky lines on the blotting paper. Had they simply shot Durrell where he stood, or had they provoked him into trying to draw? Had Marsh had the sense to keep his hands off Miss Jenny? What if Marsh had lost his head and killed her?

There was a sudden, urgent hammering on his office door. Sharpe jumped, snapping the pencil.

'What is it?'

The door opened and one of the bartenders poked his head into the room.

'That Jonah Durrell's just come back into town leading three hosses with bodies strapped across them!' the barkeep said excitedly.

Sharpe froze for a moment, unable to breathe, then a heady mix of hate, anger and fear swept through him. He lunged to his feet and headed through the door, brushing past the barkeep without a word.

The saloon had half-emptied, men crowding at the door and windows to watch as Jonah drove a buggy along the street. Miss Jenny sat beside him, and three horses followed the buggy with bodies tied over their saddles. Sharpe forced his way through the crowd in the doorway until he could see clearly for himself. He barely glanced at the bodies, recognizing them as the men he had sent out, or at Jenny. His attention was centred on Jonah Durrell.

Durrell, as fresh and smart as when he'd set out that morning. Durrell, handsome, and still by Jenny's side.

Sharpe's right hand dropped to the butt of his Colt revolver, his fingers finding their place on the grips while his eyes remained locked on Jonah Durrell as the buggy passed. Every muscle in his body was rigid with tension as Durrell passed without glancing at the saloon. Sharpe's breath came fast and rapid as he battled with the urge to draw and kill. Only when the buggy had passed, so Sharpe could no longer see the people inside, did he draw a deep breath and lift his hand away from his gun.

The people pressing around him were talking loudly, discussing the bodies tied over the horses, and Jonah and Miss Jenny being together. Sharpe elbowed his way back through the crowd to the relative peace of his saloon. He wiped his sweaty palm on the leg of his pants as he made his way to the bar, and ordered a shot of whiskey. Sharpe slugged the drink down and shivered. The barkeep poured another and looked at him questioningly. Sharpe was in no mood to talk; he barely trusted himself to speak evenly. Turning away from the polished bar, he stared moodily at the people scattered about the room.

At first he barely knew what he was looking at, but as the surge of hatred began to ebb, Sharpe started looking at people more clearly. He automatically assessed the number of patrons, the type of drinks being served, which games were busy and the way the girls were acting with customers. It was the routine of a good manager and the familiar problems brought Sharpe's mind back into focus. Men were returning to the bar now, so Sharpe moved away to make room for them. As he strolled across the saloon, he found his attention drawn to one of his girls, Maybelline.

She was perched on the knee of a mine engineer, laughing at a joke he was telling. Even she brought Jonah to Sharpe's mind, for she was the girl Barker had used as an excuse for picking a fight with the manhunter. '*I can't stand to hear a man badmouthing a woman,*' Durrell had said afterwards. And Durrell was always defensive towards Miss Jenny and her whores. Sharpe looked at Maybelline thought-fully, fiddling with the silver ring on his right hand. He had a feeling he knew how to get Jonah Durrell off guard.

10

Jonah Durrell was mentally and physically tired as he left Miss Jenny's place that night, but it was a good feeling. The cool, night air seemed rather colder to him after the warmth of the parlour-house, so he strode rapidly along the sidewalk towards his hotel. After giving Marshal Tapton a detailed account of the attack by the bandits, Jonah had returned with Jenny to her place. The knowledge that the man who had murdered Miss Lucy was now dead had brought an abrupt feeling of relief to the girls, leading to an impromptu party with Jonah as the guest of honour.

Jonah smiled to himself as he thought back to the evening's activities. A good meal, wine, and some dancing in the limited space available to start with. Then he'd whisked Miss Tania upstairs for a Brazilian language lesson of the 'show and tell' variety, in which he'd learnt a lot of words he suspected were not usually found in English-Brazilian dictionaries. When he'd recovered sufficiently from that, he'd coaxed Miss Sandy away from the piano with the suggestion that she play with his instrument for a while. As expected, Miss Sandy was quite a virtuoso, leaving him too tired to manage an encore. After another drink downstairs, he'd made his farewells and left, intending to get a good night's sleep.

The rest of the town had pretty much settled down for the night. The saloons had closed their doors, low lights glimmering in the windows as staff tidied up. A solitary bay horse stood hipshot outside the pool hall further up Panhandle Street. As Jonah crossed the street, the only sounds were a burro braying somewhere, and the ever-present pounding of the mills. He turned down the alley beside the Colorado Hotel, intending to visit his horse in the stable back of the hotel, as he usually did last thing. Jonah yawned, keeping an eye out for the piles of trash and horse manure that were hard to see in the darkness between buildings. He had almost reached the stable when he heard a woman's voice, crying out in distress.

Jonah immediately came alert, unfastening his overcoat without thinking, to have free access to his guns. The cry was repeated, not far away to his left.

'Stop! Stop it!'

Jonah turned and sprinted towards the sound, passing between the darkened land office and the back of the saloon. Ahead, on open ground, he could see two dark figures struggling together. The shorter one wore a cloak, and the other had a man's broad-brimmed hat. Drawing his right-hand gun, Jonah emerged from the alley.

'Let her go!' he ordered, lifting the Smith & Wesson.

The taller figure swung around and shoved the woman hard in Jonah's direction. She staggered towards him, squealing in fear, and tripped. The man was fleeing, heading to Panhandle Street without looking back. Jonah made a split-second decision and moved to catch the woman as she fell. She gasped as he caught her, just above the ground. Jonah lowered her down carefully, glanced in the direction of the now-vanished assailant, and holstered his gun.

'Are you hurt, miss?' he asked, crouching down to face the woman.

The wide hood of her cloak threw a shadow across her face. All Jonah could readily see was some blonde hair that tumbled out of the hood to shine in the faint light. The cloak was open enough to show him the front of a low-cut dress, which with the smell of perfume, beer and tobacco, told him that she was one of the town's many saloon-girls.

'My ankle. I've hurt my ankle,' she whispered, extending her left leg.

'Did he hit you?' Jonah asked, peering at the shadowy face.

She turned her face away from him

as she shook her head. 'No, he just shook me.' Her voice was oddly high-pitched, but somehow sounded familiar. Jonah puzzled over it for a moment as he turned his attention to her ankle.

She wore high-heeled boots that covered her legs to halfway up her shapely calves. Jonah lifted her leg gently. 'Can you move your toes?'

She tried, and gave a little gasp. Jonah felt her ankle carefully, making her shudder. He couldn't help noticing that each shudder had an interesting effect on the cleavage visible between the folds of the cloak. In the dim light, Jonah could just see a dark spot above one breast. It was a beauty spot he'd seen before, and only a few days ago. Jonah forgot about her ankle for a moment as he tried to recall the meeting.

His thoughts were shattered by a stealthy sound from close behind. Jonah started to rise and turn. He felt, rather than saw, a sudden movement from someone standing behind him. Then a heavy blow at the back of his head sent him sprawling to the ground. Jonah hit the dirt and lay still, eyes closed, barely able to summon a conscious thought or movement. Someone booted him hard in the ribs. Jonah simply lay as he'd fallen, rocking slightly with the blow.

Someone grabbed his arm, his coat, rolling him onto his back. Hands fumbled at his gunbelt, releasing the buckle and pulling the belt clear of his unresisting body. Snatches of voices came through the fog in his brain.

'Boss wants to see these.'

'You, gal, get on out of here.'

'Quick, we gotta dump him afore anyone comes along.'

Two pairs of hands lifted Jonah roughly, swaying him as the men moved. Their footsteps changed in sound, now clomping on wooden boards that sounded hollow underneath. Something in Jonah's dazed mind warned him of imminent danger. Something about the sound of running water nearby. Jonah moaned softly and tried to open his eyes. The men grunted as they hoisted him up and swung him out. Jonah gasped, sucking in cold air as he fell. Then he hit the icy water of the river, and sank.

For the first few moments, Jonah lost consciousness entirely. The next thing he knew, he was suffocating, his nose and mouth full of water. Barely aware of what he was doing, Jonah started to swim. He kicked his way to the surface, gasping and coughing as he reached the air. At first, it was all he could do to stay afloat and let himself be carried along in the current. Jonah blinked water from his eyes, still gasping, and forced himself to think. The Animas wasn't very deep or fast, but his muscles were weak and rubbery. The icy water was sapping what little strength he had and his clothes were weighing him down. Already Jonah was so low in the water that it was lapping at his chin.

Jonah managed to struggle out of his

unfastened overcoat, getting another mouthful of water as he pulled it off. He let himself float upright as he coughed, trying to clear his lungs. He was so cold his hands were too numb to unfasten his jacket. Jonah fought down panic and forced himself to think. As he looked to the banks, one foot touched a rock in the riverbed. Jonah's heart lifted at the knowledge that the river wasn't as deep as he'd feared. He struck out at an angle, aiming for the left bank. The current bullied him downstream but he got closer. Jonah found he was gasping for breath, light-headed from the effort. He stopped swimming and let his feet drop, feeling for the riverbed.

He touched bottom and stood up; the water reached halfway up his chest. Jonah surged forward, reaching for the willows and shrubs that edged the banks. The water swept him off his feet, submerging him once again. Jonah flailed about, fighting his way to the surface. His chest was heaving as he forced his way onwards, half-swimming, half-walking. The willow came within reach, but he couldn't make his outstretched hand grasp the slender branch. The water was shallower here, and Jonah stood for a few moments, sobbing for breath, before trying again. This time he seized the branch and hauled himself from the river.

Jonah scrambled up the bank and through the scrub before his legs buckled and he collapsed. He lay as he'd fallen, surrendering to the pain in his head and the desperate exhaustion. Water ran from his hair across his face and down his neck. Every inch of his clothing was soaked in the icy mountain river water. His frantic gasping had barely eased before the violent shivering began. Jonah moaned softly to himself. Slowly, he forced himself first to his hands and knees, then to his feet. He swayed and nearly fell. The temptation to let himself collapse and give in to the fogginess was immense. Somehow, Jonah found the willpower to start walking.

★　★　★

Miss Jenny covered a yawn as she took a last look at the parlour rooms. There was a fair amount of mess for the staff to clear up in the morning, but all glasses and dishes had been returned to the kitchen and the furniture was more or less in the right places.

'It was one swell night, wasn't it, Miss Jenny?' remarked Albert Hudson, the doorman. He usually did the last rounds of the evening with her before retiring to the small room he shared with the cook.

'It was,' she agreed, extinguishing the crystal-shaded lamp by the door of the music-parlour. 'It's been a hell of a long day, and I guess we'll all sleep like logs tonight.'

Albert smiled. 'I'm sure aiming to . . .'

His comment was cut off by a banging on the front door. Three steady thuds, and after a pause, another, softer one. Jenny glanced at Albert, who was

166

holding a lamp in the darkened rooms. As they waited there were two more knocks on the door and a voice, not loud enough to be understood.

'We'd better go see,' Jenny said quietly, moving forwards.

Albert moved in front, gesturing for her to stay behind him. Jenny obeyed, taking the lantern as the black man unbolted the door and opened it cautiously.

At first, neither of them saw anyone, then they looked down to see the slumped form huddled on the doorstep.

'Jonah!' Jenny was the first to recognize the bedraggled, shivering man. She reached out to help him up and recoiled from the feel of his cold, wet clothes. 'What's happened? Are you hurt?'

With Albert's help, she got Jonah up and helped him through to the kitchen at the back of the house. The cook, Ken, was still awake, and came to see what was happening. As soon as Jonah had been lowered into a chair beside the range, Jenny grabbed a cloth to dry his hair as she issued orders for towels and blankets. Jonah was shivering but otherwise silent and lethargic as they stripped off his wet clothes and wrapped him in towels and blankets. He moaned when Jenny briskly rubbed the back of his head. She stopped immediately, and looked closely at the dark hair.

'There's a bruise coming here, and the skin's split,' she said, gently supporting his lolling head. 'He's taken a plumb nasty blow from something.'

'Or someone,' suggested Albert, who was busy rubbing Jonah's legs with a towel. 'Cracked him on the head and dumped him in the river, most like.' His brisk movement slowed as he turned to look at the heap of wet clothing that Ken was transferring to the sink. 'They gone and stole his gunbelt.'

Jenny looked up sharply: she hadn't noticed the absence of the gunbelt until it was pointed out. Without thinking, she caressed Jonah's cheek in sympathy.

'The coffee's hot,' Ken said, turning from the sink to the stove.

'We'll try and get some inside him,' Jenny said, turning her attention to the immediate problems. She crouched in front of Jonah, heedless of her elaborate skirts soaking up the water that had pooled under his chair. He was dry now; his skin had regained some colour and the shivering had lessened. He was still barely conscious though, his dark eyes closed. Jenny did a rapid calculation of the beds available. Two rooms were empty, but they were on the top floor, which was the coldest, and the beds had been stripped. She made up her mind.

'Albert, fill a couple of hot water bottles and tuck them in my bed, please. We'll put Jonah there when he's had some coffee.'

Half an hour later, the parlour-house was quiet, and Jenny was in her bedroom. To save on transport costs, she had had a single bed shipped over the mountains to Motherlode for her own use. Her candle showed her Jonah, deeply asleep in the middle of the bed, his hair dark against the pillow. As she looked, she saw him shiver a little, still chilled from the icy ducking. Jenny stripped off her clothes, blew out the candle, and slipped into the bed beside him, trying not to let any cold air under the quilt and blankets.

As Jonah was lying in the middle of the bed, there was very little room left for Jenny. She moved Jonah's arm without disturbing him as he slept on. He shifted without waking, twining himself against her. In spite of her awkward position, Jenny found herself comforted by his proximity. It was a long time since a man had slept in her bed. She liked the feel of his skin against hers, the muscular heaviness of him. It was the feeling, however fleeting, of companionship. As her body warmed his, Jenny relaxed and slept.

11

Adam Sharpe sat and gazed at the gunbelt spread across his desk. It was a beautiful piece of work, the black leather gleaming in the morning sunlight from the window. Sharpe unholstered one of the matched Smith & Wessons and held it up, admiring the scrolled fancy-work etched into the revolver. He cocked the hammer, appreciating the smooth action, and smiled to himself. This was a fine trophy. Sharpe longed to strap the gunbelt on again, as he had last night when it had been given to him, and to regain the sense of power and success it gave him. Carefully lowering the hammer, he holstered the revolver and caressed the leather again. Not here though, not yet. It wouldn't do to be seen wearing this distinctive gunbelt.

A timid knocking on his office door disturbed the saloon-keeper's thoughts.

'Who is it?' he called, ready to move his prize out of sight.

'Maybelline.' The voice was soft.

Sharpe told her to enter, leaving the gunbelt displayed on his desk. The saloon-girl approached the desk, taking the chair that Sharpe gestured her to. Although she wore her bright, flouncy saloon dress, her heart-shaped face was downcast beneath the make-up.

'You done a fine job last night,' Sharpe told her pleasantly. 'I'm mighty grateful for your help.' He took some bank notes from a drawer and put them on the desk beside her.

Maybelline glanced at the notes, then at the gunbelt. 'You didn't allow as you wanted him killed,' she said quietly.

Irritation punctured Sharpe's good mood. 'It's done now,' he snapped. 'That manhunter won't be interfering in my business no more. Iffen Durrell's dead, you're an accessory to it and what chance do you think a saloon-girl will have in front of a jury? There's no reason for you to kick up a fuss about last night now, is there?'

Fear flashed in the girl's eyes. She shook her head rapidly.

'Now take the money and buy yourself something pretty,' Sharpe said, softening his voice.

He watched as Maybelline scooped up the notes and pushed them down the front of her dress. She escaped from his office without looking back and Sharpe dismissed her from his mind. He was thinking about Durrell again. No one had yet reported finding the manhunter's body. Was it out of sight, washed up in some scrub? Or had it been carried downstream right out of town? Having the gunbelt wasn't enough. Sharpe needed to see Durrell's body for himself. Abruptly, he stood up and headed for the door. He would find Fossett, one of the men he'd sent after Durrell last night, and send him down river to look for the body. Sharpe wasn't going to rest easy until he'd seen Jonah Durrell in his coffin.

* ★ ★

Jonah spent the day resting quietly in bed, a necessity forced on him more by the blow to his head, than by his brush with hypothermia. Jenny had risen before he woke, so he had no idea that they'd shared a bed for the night. A stove was lit in one of the rooms upstairs, and Jonah moved there around midday, wearing bed-clothes borrowed from Albert. He walked up both flights of stairs unaided, but was glad to slide between the warmed sheets.

'How's your head?' Jenny asked, watching as he made himself comfortable.

'Aching again,' Jonah answered. 'But not so much as it was earlier.'

'Serves you right for trying to think too much.' Jenny settled herself in a chair and picked up a piece of mending she had brought with her.

When he'd woken up midmorning, Jonah had done his best to recall the

174

attack. After fretting for a while, he'd achieved nothing more than a dim memory that a girl had been involved, and a headache. Before long, he'd been forced to accept Jenny's advice to rest, and had promptly fallen asleep for two hours. Now he looked up at her as she carefully threaded a needle with white cotton.

'I owe you my life,' he said quietly.

Jenny didn't answer at once, apparently busy with her needle. When she was satisfied, she turned to him. 'And how much do I owe to you, Jonah? For the carriage? The bandits? For being concerned about what happened to Lucy? You reap what you sow. Now close your eyes and sleep while I mend this petticoat.'

Jonah smiled, and this time did as he was told without argument.

★   ★   ★

The next morning, Jonah submitted to having breakfast in bed, but insisted that he was well enough to get up afterwards.

'I'm the nearest thing to a qualified doctor in this town, and I say I'm as sound as a dollar,' he told Jenny.

'I guess it'll save the maids from running up and down two flights of stairs looking after you,' she answered flippantly, pleased by his recovery.

Jonah made an indignant face at her assumed lack of concern, and Jenny laughed.

A short while later, he joined her downstairs in her office, where she was catching up with some routine book-keeping. Settling himself in a chair, Jonah looked at the carriage clock on her desk, and took out his pocket watch. He set the hands to the right time, wound it and listened to see if it worked after being submerged in the river. After a few moments, he realized that Jenny had stopped writing and was looking at him.

'Your watch is gold, isn't it?' she asked thoughtfully.

Jonah nodded. 'Eighteen carat, like the chain. I reckon I'll have to take it to the jewellery store in Silverton and get it fixed.'

'You've got gold cufflinks, too, haven't you?'

Jonah pulled back the sleeve of his jacket to show off the cufflinks on his left arm. The wet clothes he'd arrived in had been carefully cleaned and fixed up as good as new. Being properly dressed again had raised his spirits no end.

'Yes, my cufflinks are gold too,' he said, puzzled by her questions.

'Someone attacked you, but it wasn't to rob you,' Jenny said slowly. 'They didn't take any of your valuables, or your pocketbook. They only took your gunbelt.'

'My gunbelt!' Jonah's hands dropped to his sides, where his guns usually rested. Feeling secure and sheltered during his recovery, he'd not thought about his guns beyond vaguely imagining that Jenny knew where they were. 'I thought you — ' Jonah stopped in

mid-sentence, frowning. 'No . . . they
. . . someone unfastened the belt and
pulled it off me. I couldn't do anything.
They were talking about it.'

He paused again, biting on his lower
lip as he struggled to pick out the hazy
memories. Jenny hesitated to ask
questions, afraid she would interrupt
his train of thought.

'I think there were two men,' Jonah
went on slowly. 'I think they said
something about the gunbelt. And one
of them said something to the girl.
There was a girl there, and she'd
sprained her ankle, or pretended, and
she was a saloon-girl; yes.' The words
came faster now. He wasn't looking at
Jenny; his attention was turned inwards.
'I couldn't really see her face but I'd
seen her before, here, Motherlode. She
had a . . . a spot.' Jonah touched himself
on his chest, above his heart. 'A black
. . . like a freckle.'

'A beauty spot,' Jenny said softly.

Jonah nodded. 'A beauty spot on her
left breast.' He looked up suddenly, his

eyes bright. 'She was in Sharpe's saloon! He invited me for a drink and . . . Maybelline . . . was there. We were talking when this feller came and picked a fight over her. It was the same son-of-a-bitch that threw the firecracker under your carriage.'

'His death was no loss to society and that's a fact,' Jenny said robustly. 'Do you reckon she set you up for that besides?'

Jonah thought for a moment, then shook his head. 'I don't know. She must have been part of the set-up night before last. She must have seen whoever it was coming up behind me and she didn't let on.'

Jenny raised an eyebrow and half-smiled. 'I can't think why any saloon-girl would want you dead. Jealous husbands and anxious fathers, yes, but not a saloon-girl. How many jealous men are there after your hide?'

Jonah grinned. 'None, I hope. I avoid women with gun-wielding relatives. It's not like I have a problem finding all the safe women I want,' he added smugly.

Jenny hid her amusement at his utter shamelessness. 'Vanity is a sin, you know.'

'So are lust, gluttony and sloth,' he replied promptly. 'And I enjoy all of them.'

Jenny threw a penwiper at him. 'I reckon someone should go speak to this Maybelline. And not you,' she added. 'Whichever snake she's working with wants you dead. You'd be as dumb as a shovel if you went walking out on Panhandle Street where anyone could see you.'

'I'd be naked without my guns,' Jonah said bitterly. 'I'd like to speak to Maybelline myself though. If someone's been using her to get to me, she might find it plumb difficult to look me in the eyes and lie.'

Jenny nodded. 'We'll get her here,' she promised.

★   ★   ★

Maybelline felt herself trembling a little with excitement and fear as she followed Miss Jenny's cook in through the back door of the parlour-house. Excitement at the sudden summons from the madam and the possibility of leaving the noisy saloon for a fine parlour-house. Fear at the thought of leaving behind what she knew, and of how Sharpe would react to her defection.

Ken led her through two doors and into the public section of the parlour-house. Maybelline drew in a breath of pleasure at the flowered paper on the walls, the polished wood of the staircase and the air of elegance and comfort, so different to the saloon. She could hear the sounds of vigorous sweeping and cushion thumping from the parlours at the front of the house, and women talking upstairs, but there was no time to take in these things. Ken knocked on a door, and stood aside to let her into Miss Jenny's office. Maybelline took a moment to fluff out her hair, and entered.

Miss Jenny was sitting behind a desk,

wearing an elegant, silver-grey day-dress, simply trimmed with black velvet ribbon. Maybelline unconsciously adjusted her shawl to cover more of her garish saloon clothes, and managed a smile.

'Good morning, Maybelline,' Miss Jenny said, her voice and face inexpressive.

'Hello, Maybelline,' added another voice, from behind the saloon girl.

Maybelline squealed in surprise and whirled around, her eyes wide. 'Jonah!'

The manhunter stepped forward from his place beside the door, half-smiling at her. 'Large as life and twice as ugly. As the saying goes,' he added, shamelessly disassociating himself from any suggestion of ugliness.

Maybelline stared at him for a moment, then her face broke into a wide smile. 'Oh I'm so glad you're all right,' she said impulsively.

'What should be wrong with me?' Jonah asked, losing the air of good-humour.

Maybelline floundered, unsure of how much Jonah already knew. 'I . . . er

182

. . . you haven't been seen around town for a couple of days.'

'I've been recovering from the bang on the head your accomplice gave me,' Jonah said bluntly. 'Just before I got thrown into the Animas to drown or freeze.'

'I didn't know they were going to kill you!' Maybelline blurted out. 'It was just to get your guns; to make you look a fool. I swear I didn't know it was anything more than that. You were nice to me,' she finished pleadingly.

Jonah's eyes softened a little but Maybelline's ordeal wasn't over yet.

'Who was behind it?' he asked. 'Who wanted my guns?'

Maybelline squirmed and fidgeted with her shawl, her eyes on the rug. She started when Miss Jenny spoke, having forgotten the other woman's presence.

'Are you scared to tell us, Maybelline?' Miss Jenny asked softly.

Maybelline turned to look at her, struggled for words, and made a small nod.

Jonah moved to the side of the desk and spoke again, his voice kind. 'How did they threaten you? What did they say would happen?'

Maybelline took a deep breath. 'He said that if I tried to tell the truth, no jury would believe a saloon-girl. And he said that I was an accessory to the killing.' She looked at the man and woman facing her. They were both listening intently but she found it hard to guess what they were thinking. Neither seemed angry at her. Maybelline began to feel a little less scared.

'You can't be an accessory to murder, because I didn't die,' Jonah pointed out. 'But someone wants me dead, and he's not too particular how it gets done. If you help me out, I can take steps to see he doesn't get another chance. Whoever's behind this is going to be dead or behind bars when I catch up with him, and I will, because that's what I'm good at. Either way, he won't be able to hurt you. If you won't help, you increase the risk that he gets to me, before I get to him. If you tell, I can keep both of us safe.'

It seemed a lot for one man to promise. Maybelline knew that Sharpe had plenty of money, and could call on several thugs and gunmen to do his dirty work. But then, Maybelline had seen Jonah beat up on Barker. He'd also killed those three bandits who'd attacked him in the woods. Maybelline suddenly wondered whether Sharpe had sent those men after Jonah; she'd seen at least one of them in the private areas of the saloon. She made up her mind suddenly.

'It was Sharpe,' she said, looking Jonah in the eyes. 'I don't know why he wants you dead. Those bandits that attacked you out of town — I saw one of them in back of the saloon, round about Sharpe's office.'

Jonah and Jenny looked at one another; it was clear that neither of them had expected this.

'What did I ever do to Sharpe?' Jonah asked plaintively.

'Apart from showing up in Mother-lode and spoiling his role as the town's most handsome, best-dressed, high-earning and all-round eligible man?' Jenny asked.

'Well that, obviously,' Jonah agreed with a brief grin. 'But I'm damned sure there's more to it than that.'

'I don't care too hard why he wants you dead,' Jenny said. 'So long as we know who it is, we can figure out what we're going to do about it.' She turned to the saloon-girl. 'I reckon you'd best go on back to the Silver Lode before anyone gets to wondering too much about where you've got to.'

Maybelline nodded eagerly. 'I won't tell 'bout you being here, Jonah,' she promised. 'I'm mighty glad you ain't dead.' Her pretty face had come to life again as it had sunk in that she no longer needed to feel guilty about a man she'd lured to his death.

'I'm mighty glad too,' Jonah answered with a smile. He stepped forward, and to Maybelline's flustered delight, took her hand and kissed it gracefully.

She gawped at him for a moment, then as he released her hand, she pulled herself together. Bobbing a quick curtsey to Miss Jenny, Maybelline left the office.

Leaving through the back of the parlour-house, Maybelline hurried along behind the meat market and the post office, before heading back onto Panhandle Street. A couple of minutes later she was back in the Silver Lode, which was fairly quiet at this hour. One of the bartenders called to her.

'Sharpe's been looking for you. He wants you in his office, pronto.'

Maybelline took a moment to shake the dust from her clothes, and to catch her breath, then headed for Sharpe's office.

When she entered, he was sitting behind his desk, gazing at Jonah's gunbelt, spread in front of him. Maybelline approached, trying to make herself look calm. Sharpe looked up, saw the shawl she still wore, and frowned.

'Where've you been?' he demanded.

'I went to the post office; there was a letter for me.' Maybelline gave the excuse she'd planned earlier. 'It was real busy in there.'

Much to her relief, Sharpe merely grunted and told her that as she'd arrived late, she would have to work later into the evening shift. His attention returned to the gunbelt in front of him. Sharpe gazed at it for so long that Maybelline began to wonder if he'd forgotten her presence. She shifted her weight and coughed.

'Where in hell is he?' Sharpe muttered.

He looked up suddenly, startling Maybelline with the intensity of his gaze. 'What the hell's happened to him? I've had men searching up and down the Animas but there's no sign of him. He's not been to his hotel room, or to see his hoss. It's like Durrell's vanished!' Sharpe thumped the desk for emphasis.

Maybelline watched him warily, but

didn't dare say anything.

Sharpe continued, 'I've thought of someplace else to try though. Durrell was making up to Miss Jenny, and she was fool enough to be taken in by his snake-oil patter. If there's anyone in this two-shanty town who knows where Durrell is, it's Miss Jenny.'

'Miss Jenny?' Maybelline squeaked.

Sharpe stared at her, his eyes hard and cold. 'Why do you sound so surprised?'

Maybelline felt herself starting to panic under Sharpe's scrutiny. All she could think of was the importance of keeping the secret. She fidgeted around on the spot as she tried to think of a good answer.

'Well, I thought Jonah was dead. I heard him go in the river; I heard the splash. How could he be at Miss Jenny's?'

Sharpe stood up, his eyes still fixed on her like a hunter stalking its prey. 'You reckon he's *at* Miss Jenny's?' he asked slowly.

'No!' Maybelline blurted out. She could feel her face getting redder as she got more flustered. 'I never said he was at Miss Jenny's. You said he was.'

'I said she might know where he is,' Sharpe corrected, moving around the desk. 'Why are you acting like a cat on hot coals, Maybelline?'

She gazed at him like a rabbit transfixed by a fox.

'Is Jonah Durrell at Miss Jenny's place?' Sharpe demanded.

Maybelline shook her head.

Sharpe lashed out with a stinging slap to her face, bringing a cry of shock and pain.

'Is Durrell at Miss Jenny's place?' He yelled at her from so close that Maybelline felt spittle hit her face.

She sobbed in fear; afraid to look at Sharpe, and afraid to look away.

This time Sharpe punched her, hard enough to knock her back a couple of steps. Maybelline held her hand against her mouth, tasting blood as it oozed from a split lip.

'Is that where you were this morning?' Sharpe hissed. 'I was looking for you to send you there, to find him, but you knew he was there all along.'

'I didn't know,' Maybelline wailed. She saw Sharpe clench his fist again and threw up her hands to protect herself. 'They sent for me! Jonah remembered seeing me before they attacked him. I swear, I didn't know he was alive until this morning.'

'Durrell's at Miss Jenny's place now?' Sharpe demanded to know.

Maybelline nodded once, and started to cry.

12

Sharpe turned away from her. After a moment of awful stillness, he snatched a water-glass from his desk and hurled it across the room. It hit the far wall and exploded into shards.

'Goddam that whore!' Sharpe yelled. He swung back and forth across the room as he ranted, apparently oblivious to Maybelline's presence. 'I knew that whore-begotten bitch was working against me. Durrell won't get his hands on her and that fancy parlour-house. He's done nothing but stick himself into my plans right from the get-go. I'm gonna make sure of you this time, Durrell; you can't shoot your way past all the guns I can hire. And Miss Jenny can sell up or die.'

Sharpe stormed from the room without looking back.

Maybelline sniffed once and wiped

her face with a corner of her shawl. Sharpe's outburst had terrified her, and she felt swamped with the misery of having betrayed Jonah once again. She found herself looking at Jonah's gunbelt, still spread across Sharpe's desk. An idea flashed into her head, and she acted at once. Hurrying forward, Maybelline whipped off her shawl and picked up the heavy gunbelt. She slung it around her shoulders, so the holsters hung under her arms. After a short, anxious struggle, she managed to get the ends roughly buckled behind her back, so they didn't hang down, and covered everything with her shawl.

Maybelline hurried to the office window and heaved up the sash. A quick glance showed no one in the alley between the saloon and Middleton's Hardware Emporium. Maybelline hitched herself through the window, grateful that her skirts weren't so long as a respectable woman's would be. Once outside, she ran across the open ground to the laundry, and along behind the buildings lining

Panhandle Street until she was opposite Miss Jenny's. Using a delivery wagon outside The Shovel as cover, Maybelline studied the street carefully before nipping across and making her way to the back of the parlour-house.

★ ★ ★

Jonah and Jenny were still conferring in her office when Maybelline was shown in. Jonah saw her split and puffy lips, and stood up to give his chair to her.

'What happened? Was it Sharpe?' he asked, a hard light coming into his eyes.

Maybelline nodded, gazing gratefully at him as he knelt beside her. Miss Jenny was giving rapid orders to Ken, asking for hot water and a cloth. Maybelline told her story to Jonah, clinging to the hand he'd offered her. Jonah's face grew darker as he listened to the retelling of Sharpe's threats.

'No one's blaming you,' he told the girl, seeing the tears come back to her

194

eyes. 'You did the right thing, coming here to tell us.'

'We've got to make some decisions fast,' Miss Jenny interrupted, coming forward with water and cloth to tend to the girl's face. She gently wiped the blood away as she spoke. 'If Sharpe's coming here with gunmen, we've got to be ready for him.'

'It's me he wants dead. I'll get out and keep him away from here,' Jonah said, standing up.

Jenny shook her head. 'Sharpe wants me to sell up to him or die. I don't aim to do either. You couldn't take on him and his men alone, even if you had your Smith & Wessons.'

Maybelline gave a sudden squeak, and threw back her shawl. 'I got your guns,' she exclaimed. 'Sharpe had them in his office so I took them for you.'

A huge smile lit up Jonah's face as he saw his gunbelt draped around her shoulders. 'Clever girl!' he said, giving her a kiss on the cheek before reaching to take the belt. He swiftly strapped the black leather gunbelt into place and carefully examined each revolver in turn.

'I'll see what other weapons we've got, and tell everyone what's going on,' Jenny said.

Within five minutes, nearly everyone in the parlour-house had assembled in the public dining-room. Maybelline was at the window in the front parlour, keeping watch through the lacy curtains. Ken was in his kitchen, a shotgun propped next to the sink as he scrubbed potatoes. The young maids had been sent to the marshal's office, with orders to stay there until someone came to fetch them. All ten working girls, with Albert in their midst, listened intently to Jonah as he swiftly explained the situation. Two girls were still in their wrappers; others were wearing plain, off-duty dresses. None had yet applied make-up or styled their hair. Jonah spoke seriously to the women before him, noting the assortment of shotguns, derringers and cheap revolvers they held.

'Anyone who doesn't want to get

involved in a shooting match had better clear out quick,' he finished. 'This is a serious business.'

There was a rustle of movement as the women looked at one another and started to make their decisions. Miss Sandy was the first to speak.

'You said that the bandits who attacked you in the woods had been sent by Sharpe. Well, one of them was the man who killed Lucy. Maybe Sharpe was behind that too.'

Her suggestion brought shocked comments from the others.

'Why would he do something like that?' asked Miss Helen.

'He wants me to sell up to him,' Jenny reminded them. 'The first time he came here was after Lucy's murder, and he was asking then if I felt safe here.'

'I bet my bottom dollar he's been behind all the trouble here,' Miss Megan exclaimed, lifting the old revolver she carried.

Jonah spoke up to stop the developing conversation. 'We may not have much time. You have to decide if you're going to stay here or go someplace safer.'

Miss Erica spoke first. 'You and Miss Jenny are staying here to fight Sharpe, aren't you?' When Jonah and Jenny both nodded, Erica continued. 'Then I'm staying too. Miss Jenny helped me feel like a person again, not just a common whore.'

'Me too,' from Megan, Felicity and other girls.

Jonah glanced at Jenny and saw a flush of embarrassed pride on her face.

'Is anyone leaving?' he asked.

No one answered or moved. Jonah smiled briefly before turning serious again.

'Any of you who face an armed man with a gun of your own, you've got to be prepared to pull that trigger. You have to shoot to kill, to take a man's life in a nasty, messy way.' He saw the excitement leaving their faces as his words sank in and suddenly wondered if he'd lost their support. 'I wanted you to know that,' he went on, looking into each woman's eyes in turn. 'If it comes to the moment and you panic, you'll be dead before you know what's happened.'

There was a few moments silence before Miss Tania spoke up in her lilting accent, 'I killed a man before in Brazil. He deserved it too.'

The rich scorn in her voice broke the tense atmosphere and brought a ripple of laughter. Jonah let out a silent sigh of relief. It was short-lived however. The next moment, a sudden yell came from the kitchen, and the crash of glass shattering.

Jonah spun around and raced through the door into the kitchen, drawing both guns as he went. He saw Ken, wounded, his back to the wall between the door and the sink. The cook was raising his shotgun towards the shattered side window. Jonah turned towards the window, just as the back door burst open.

'Look out!' He whirled round, firing both guns at once. The man forcing his way in screamed and crashed to the floor. There was a gunshot from behind him. Jonah heard a squeal from one of the women, barely audible over the answering shots from his own guns.

'Get into the other back rooms. Defend those!' It was Jenny's voice, clear and surprisingly calm as she gave orders.

The attackers had fallen back from the door now but the body of the first gunman was slumped on the threshold. Jonah caught Ken's eye.

'How bad is it?'

The cook's brown shirt was stained with blood on his left side, but he was holding his shotgun steadily as he watched the side window.

'Nasty graze across my ribs,' Ken answered. 'Reckon it'll hurt some later.'

Helen, Annie and Coral were clustered at the back of the room, sensibly staying out of the line of fire from the windows.

'Get him out of the way so we can get that door barred,' Jonah said, gesturing to the body.

Helen started forward first, followed by Coral. As they cautiously approached the door, Jonah got closer to the window over the sink. From there, he could see most of the yard between the parlour-house and the large barn out back. Scanning the area, Jonah noticed that the double doors to the carriage-house were slightly open; those doors faced directly across the yard to the kitchen. Just out of sight to the left was a shanty used for storage, with the outhouse hidden behind it.

Miss Helen had got within reach of the body, using the kitchen door as cover. She visibly steeled herself to take hold of an outflung wrist, and to start hauling the corpse into the room. Miss Coral reached around to help her, while Ken readied himself to slam the door closed. Miss Annie had got hold of a broom and was using it to collect the Colt the dead man had dropped, while keeping herself away from the door. Their efforts were disturbed by a sudden outbreak of shots from the other side of the yard.

Jonah heard one of the other windows shatter, and the crack of a rifle from the room next to the kitchen. He moved sideways, trying to see what was happening on the left of the yard. On the far side of the window, Ken was slamming the door closed. As he looked left, Jonah glimpsed movement in the double doors of the carriage-house directly ahead of him. He ducked back, yelling a warning.

'Stay down!'

The yell was almost lost in the noise as a bullet smashed through a pane in the kitchen window, just inches from where Jonah's head had been. He closed his eyes, trying to turn his face away as glass exploded inwards. Jonah felt a sharp sting on his face and right hand, but within a second or two, he knew he wasn't badly hurt. One of the women was anxiously calling his name. Jonah opened his eyes again and smiled reassuringly, in spite of the warm blood sliding down his cheek.

'We've got the advantage here,' he

said calmly. 'They've got to come across open ground to get to us. And the longer this goes on, the more likely that Tapton and his deputy will come along and show them Judge Colt.'

Over in the carriage-house, Sharpe was thinking along the same lines. The sudden attack had nearly worked but he hadn't expected the spirited defence. They'd lost Manry to Durrell's fast shooting, and had retreated back into cover. When he got his hands on Maybelline, he was going to beat her black and blue for lighting out with Durrell's gunbelt, and then give her to his men to play with.

Sharpe stirred himself, looking at the four men in the carriage-house with him. Two more of his men were sheltering behind the store-shed in the yard. They were watching him, waiting for orders.

'It's a bunch of women in there,' he told them, gesturing to the back of the parlour-house with his Colt. 'They ain't fighters. They ain't gonna risk their pretty skins, getting all shot up for the sake of some bounty man and their madam. They're whores, they don't care two cents about who they pay their rent to, or any man who ain't paying them to open their legs.'

Fossett chuckled, licking his scarred lips. 'I'd surely like to have one of them doves open her legs for me. Them's the finest flock I seen in a long time.'

'They'll be plenty to go around when we're in there.' Sharpe's face took on an unpleasant look as he thought of having Jenny in his bed, forcing her to submit to his will. He made himself concentrate on the immediate problem: how to get across the yard to the house.

Sharpe peered through the gap between the double doors. There were four windows at the back of the parlour-house. Each probably had armed defenders, but the biggest danger was Durrell, who could only be in one place at a time. Sharpe guessed that the manhunter would most likely stay in the kitchen, to defend the door there.

'How're we gonna get to 'em?' Sturges asked.

'We go out the side door of the stables, across to that store shanty, behind it, and round to the side of the building,' Sharpe said, gauging his ideas as he spoke them. 'Deane and Garland: you stay here and keep them in the kitchen busy. They won't find it easy to shoot towards that store without showing themselves in the window. Once we're round the side of the house, there's only the women in that corner room to worry about. They'll most likely run soon as we start coming in through the window.' He looked at the two men he'd picked to stay. 'Start shooting when I give the word. There's a fifty dollar bonus for whoever finishes Durrell.'

The men grinned at him, and Garland made a throat-cutting gesture.

'Lead me to them doves!' Fossett exclaimed, laughing.

★   ★   ★

Jenny was watching the yard from the rear window of the private parlour. It was where the girls and staff ate and relaxed when not working. Now though, the atmosphere was tense. Jenny held her Winchester at the ready, Miss Megan waited beside her, clutching a short-barrelled Colt. On the far side of the window were Miss Erica with her shot-gun, and Miss Tania with a revolver in one hand and a long-bladed knife in the other. Miss Sandy was near the back of the room, holding a fancily-engraved derringer.

'Any more sign of those varmints?' Miss Sandy asked hopefully.

'Maybe they have run away already, like the yellow snakes they are,' Tania said.

Jenny answered, 'I hope not. I've had at least three window panes broken already and I sure as hell want someone to pay for it.'

Erica's reply was cut off by a sudden fusillade of gunfire from the double doors of the carriage-house. As shots crackled out in response, Jenny saw

Sharpe lead his men at a run from the end of the stable. She whipped her rifle to her shoulder and fired, shattering another pane of glass. As fast as she could, she worked the lever action and threw another shot. Then the group of men were out of sight behind the store.

'Did you hit any of them?' Erica asked, shouting to be heard over the gunfire between the other rooms and the carriage-house.

'I don't think so,' Jenny answered. Her heart was racing and her mouth was dry. It was the first time she had ever deliberately fired a gun at another person, but the group of men running across the open ground had seemed oddly unreal, like targets at a carnival side-show. Jenny forced herself to think ahead. 'They're coming in closer. They're aiming for this end of the building.'

'Can you see them?' From her position at the left of the window, Erica could see across to the stable and carriage-house, but not to the store.

She still had the air of a lady at a tea party, in spite of the businesslike way she held her shotgun.

'Not yet,' Jenny answered.

'I sure wish they'd just go away,' Miss Megan said quietly.

'So do I,' Jenny said. 'But I'll be damned before I let Sharpe force me or scare me into doing anything. If he wants to push it to a shooting match, he's gonna damn well — They're coming!'

13

Five men sprinted from behind the store to the side of the house. Jenny threw her rifle to her shoulder and hesitated, trying to choose one of the fastmoving targets. She only had a narrow angle of view as they crossed the gap between buildings. Some of them fired as they ran. More glass panes smashed as their bullets came through into the parlour. Jenny found herself firing back but the men were out of sight before she could tell if she had hit one.

Moments later there was a tremendous crash as shotgun and revolvers went off together, and the side window shattered into fragments. A man screamed, falling away from the window, but others pressed into the gap. One man poured shots into the room while another heaved up the sash window and climbed in.

Miss Megan squealed and huddled herself behind a dining chair, using that and the table for cover. She fired her revolver at the window, struggling to cock the hammer and control the recoil. Miss Erica's face was pale as she resolutely thumbed back the second hammer of her shotgun. She didn't want to hear another scream like the one after her first shot, but there was no choice now. In spite of her shakiness, the shotgun nestled firmly against her shoulder as she pulled the trigger again.

Miss Sandy fired both barrels of her derringer at the man climbing through the window, and whooped with delight as one shot hit him in the shoulder. She cracked open the little gun and started to reload it, fumbling with the cartridges. In her haste, she dropped one of the new bullets, grabbed for it, changed her mind and let it roll away. When Sandy looked up again, she saw that Fosset was through the window and heading for her. The shoulder-wound made it hard for him to lift his gun arm, but his other hand was reaching for her. Dropping the still unloaded gun, Sandy threw herself into the attack.

Miss Erica's second shot had done more damage to the window frame than to the attackers. She pressed her back against the wall as she reloaded, keeping her movements steady and deliberate. Miss Megan was having problems with her Colt, which was too large for her slender hands to cope with comfortably. The recoil was bruising her thumb, making it increasingly difficult for her to hold the gun steady when firing. She persevered, firing a shot then ducking back behind her chair to laboriously thumb the hammer back for another attempt.

As the men came through the window, Jenny was finding her rifle to be an awkward weapon for close combat. Things were happening very fast and it was difficult to get the long barrel aligned for a shot. As Fosset landed inside, she tried to aim at him and found herself pointing the gun more at Sandy. Jenny tried to correct herself, then Fosset and Sandy were too close together to risk a shot. Turning her attention back to the window, Sturges was just through and clearly intent on reaching Erica before she could reload. Jenny hastily swung the rifle around and let off a shot. It missed and ploughed into the wall, a foot from Sturges' head. Jenny flipped the lever action back and forth and tried again.

Over in the kitchen, the rapid crack of gunshots from the other side of the house was causing concern. Jonah stepped away from the window, holstering one of his guns. He broke open the other, ejecting all six used shells at once.

'I reckon there's only two in the carriage-house,' he told Ken, swiftly chambering new rounds. 'I reckon you and Albert can keep them at a safe distance.' Switching guns, he reloaded the other one.

'If they get anywhere near this

window, we'll be waiting for them,' Miss Annie promised.

Jonah nodded, giving her an approving smile. 'That's my girl.' With a gun in each hand, he headed for the door.

Sharpe scrambled through the parlour window right behind Sturges. He saw Jenny and briefly noted the other women, but his attention was for Durrell. Where was the manhunter? Dodging the struggle between Fosset and Miss Sandy, Sharpe headed for the door.

Crouching behind the table, Miss Megan fired her gun at the approaching man, only for the hammer to click on an empty chamber. She looked up at Sharpe, seeing the fierce intensity in his face as he sprinted across the parlour. Megan shivered, unwilling to attract his attention. Instead, she crawled under the table and started to reload the revolver.

As Jenny tried to get a second shot at Sturges, he turned and dropped to one knee. Her shot went over his head and into the wall. Sturges snapped off a quick shot at her in return. It tore through the curtain a few inches from Jenny's face. She jerked at the lever action, trying to reload faster than Sturges could thumb back the hammer of his Colt again. His gun tilted back smoothly and settled back into line. Jenny was still straightening her rifle. Then blood suddenly erupted from Sturges' head. The force of the short-range shotgun blast pitched him sideways. Jenny gaped at his body for a moment, her heart hammering. Her corsets suddenly seemed far too tight, and for a moment everything went grey. Then Jenny's head cleared and she saw Erica, her face white but determined as she opened her shotgun to empty the single, spent shell she'd loaded to make that vital shot.

Miss Sandy was too busy wrestling with Fosset to pay attention to the gunfire around them. She had one hand on his wrist and the other was clutching the barrel of his gun as they struggled.

Fosset tried to lift his arm upwards, out of her reach. Sandy let her knees buckle enough so her buxom weight was hanging from his arm. He dropped his arm suddenly and pulled sideways, but Sandy caught her balance quickly and went with the pull, using the motion to slam her hip against him. Fosset grunted and used his free hand to punch her in the side. Sandy's corsets absorbed most of the impact, but it was a warning. She didn't want to get hit anywhere more vulnerable.

Lowering her head suddenly, she bit hard onto the top knuckle of his right hand. Fosset yelled and tried to wrench his hand away, while lashing out wildly with his left. The blow glanced off Sandy's head, but her impetuous temper was fully roused now. She ignored the blow and bit deeper. At the same time, she twisted the gun barrel downwards. Fosset slackened his grip and Sandy tore the gun loose from his fingers. She tossed the revolver away, still holding onto him with one hand

and her teeth. Fosset was screaming curses at her, his face flushed red with fury.

He punched at her again. Sandy twisted and ducked, trying to deflect the blow with her free hand. Fosset grabbed her wrist and jerked her close against himself. He leered down at her triumphantly, getting a good eyeful of her cleavage and forgetting that he only controlled one of her hands. Sandy released his right arm and slapped him hard across the face. It startled Fosset for long enough for Sandy to bring her knee up viciously into his groin. Fosset gave a gasping cry and buckled as she snatched her other hand free. Sandy grabbed a wooden sewing box off a nearby table and smashed it into the side of his head. Fosset sprawled sideways, half-conscious. Sandy went after him, determined to keep hitting him until he stopped moving.

As the gunfire increased in the parlour, Jonah sprinted for the kitchen door. He had a gun in each hand, so Miss Coral hurried to open it for him.

Jonah slipped through the gap as the door opened, into the short passage that connected three rooms. Coming through the door at the other end was Sharpe, his Colt in hand and pointing towards Jonah. Less than twenty feet separated them as they unexpectedly faced one another. Jonah's reflexes were marginally faster. He fired his revolvers together, a split-second quicker than Sharpe.

The double impact knocked Sharpe backwards as he pulled his trigger. His bullet cracked past Jonah's ear and buried itself in the door frame. Jonah stayed frozen in place for a moment, as Sharpe fell, then blew out a sharp breath of relief. Cocking his guns, he walked forward with one gun trained on Sharpe, and the other ready in case anyone else came out of the parlour. Sharpe had dropped his gun when he fell, and Jonah carefully kicked it back towards the kitchen. There was less noise in the parlour now, and Jonah could hear Sharpe's ragged gasps as the dying man fought for breath. Jonah glanced through the door into the parlour, then turned his attention to Sharpe.

Both shots had hit the saloonkeeper in the chest. Blood was soaking through the frilly-fronted shirt, and bubbling from Sharpe's mouth. Sharpe looked up at the man looming over him, and tried to speak, but the words were lost in bright blood that choked him.

'Go ahead and curse me,' Jonah said evenly. 'There's no point saving your breath now. You won't be breathing much longer.'

The bitterness in Sharpe's eyes only softened moments before he lost consciousness. Jonah left him to die alone, and went through to the parlour.

★ ★ ★

Marshal Tapton eventually arrived when, as Miss Sandy put it, the fuss was all over and there was no danger of him breaking into a sweat. The parlour-house folk had already started to restore order; sweeping up broken glass and spent bullets. Jonah fixed up Ken's wound before helping Albert to move the bodies out to the carriage-house. Sharpe and two of his men were dead. One was badly wounded and Fosset was still concussed after his run-in with Miss Sandy. The last man to reach the parlour window had changed his mind on seeing the fierce resistance within, and had fled. The two men in the carriage-house had followed his example. Tapton took statements and viewed the bodies, getting more and more gloomy as he saw the necessary paperwork increasing. He got very little sympathy.

* * *

Two days later, Jonah Durrell called by the parlour-house on his way out of Motherlode. Jenny and her girls came out onto the sidewalk to make their farewells. They clustered around him like bright butterflies, ribbons and ruffles fluttering in the light breeze.

'You must take care of yourself,' Miss Helen insisted, her sweet face full of concern.

Jonah kissed her cheek and promised to stay alert. 'I like my skin too much to get careless about it.'

'You will be coming back to Motherlode soon, won't you?' Miss Erica asked.

Jonah smiled at the Englishwoman. 'I'm only leaving to earn more money to spend on you all.'

His gallant remark ended in a squawk as mischievous fingers tickled his ribs. Jonah turned to look down at Miss Annie, whose round eyes were brimming with wicked humour.

'There ought to be a bounty out on you, you troublemaker,' he told her with mock severity, before bending down to hug her overflowing figure.

The last farewell was for Jenny. Jonah stopped in front of her and smiled.

'The handsomest manhunter in Colorado at your service, ma'am.'

'Only in Colorado?' Jenny teased. She gently touched a scab on his cheekbone, where a shard of window glass had been embedded. 'I hope this won't damage your beauty too much.'

'I'm going to tell women that it's a duelling scar,' Jonah announced shamelessly. He took Jenny's hand and placed a delicate kiss on her fingers. As she gasped softly, he released her and stepped back to sweep his hat off and bow elegantly to the women. Replacing the hat, Jonah jumped lightly from the sidewalk, and vaulted into the saddle of his waiting horse. With a last, brilliant smile, he urged his horse into a gallop, weaving along the busy street, and was soon out of sight. Miss Jenny sighed: Motherlode would seem a much drabber place until he returned.

We do hope that you have enjoyed reading this large print book.

Did you know that all of our titles are available for purchase?

We publish a wide range of high quality large print books including:
Romances, Mysteries, Classics
General Fiction
Non Fiction and Westerns

Special interest titles available in large print are:
The Little Oxford Dictionary
Music Book, Song Book
Hymn Book, Service Book

Also available from us courtesy of Oxford University Press:
Young Readers' Dictionary
(large print edition)
Young Readers' Thesaurus
(large print edition)

For further information or a free brochure, please contact us at:
Ulverscroft Large Print Books Ltd.,
The Green, Bradgate Road, Anstey,
Leicester, LE7 7FU, England.
Tel: (00 44) **0116 236 4325**
Fax: (00 44) **0116 234 0205**

Other titles in the
Linford Western Library:

ESCAPE FROM FORT BENTON

Scott Connor

Nathan Palmer and Jeff Morgan happen across the victim of an ambush. The dying man gives them a cryptic message about ten thousand dollars being available in Fort Benton in five days' time. However, arriving at Fort Benton to get the money, they come up against Mayor Decker and his ruthless form of justice. Soon the pair are beaten up and thrown in jail. In Decker's clutches, they're going to need all their courage if they are ever to escape.

TRAITOR'S GOLD

Wade Dellman

Marshal Dave Stevens' mission was to capture the outlaw Ned Bartell, a traitor who had caused the deaths of two thousand of his fellow Confederate soldiers during the Civil War. Pinkerton operative Marie Devlin, whose dead brother Bartell had betrayed, and ex-army veteran Thorpe also wanted Bartell brought to justice. Bartell's greed for gold brought Stevens, Thorpe and the girl together — but would their combined resolve still be enough to ensure their survival against the vicious outlaws?